Mausoleum Madness

A JESSAMY WARD MYSTERY

PENELOPE CRESS, STEVE HIGGS

Contents

What Friends Are For

"Excuse me, this is my office I believe!"

"Sorry, Vicar. Dr Sam and your sister said you'd given them permission." My embarrassed parish secretary made a show of shooing both my duplicitous friend and my deceitful sibling from my desk.

"Barbara Graham, you are as rich as your fruit cake! Don't try to pin this on us." My best friend Sam strolled around to the front of the mahogany desk and lifted her skinny rear end onto its green leather top. She crossed her long legs with all the confidence one would expect from the local hospital's chief surgeon. "Ms. Graham is as much a part of this intervention as we are."

"Intervention?" I asked, trying my best not to smile. I wanted to convey a sense of righteous indignation at their wanton abuse of my workspace.

"Yes. Intervention. Dear sister, you know I have long admired your arrogant disregard of fashion trends, but you aren't a lowly curate anymore. You are the head honcho around here and you need to start dressing the part."

"Zuzu, have you looked in the mirror lately? You are the last person who should be dispensing sartorial advice." My sister Zuzu, or Susannah as she was named by my parents, arrived only yesterday sporting a rucksack of dirty t-shirts and underwear, the jeans

1

she was wearing, a moth-eaten blue sweater and a bright yellow anorak. Her naturally blonde hair was loosely scooped up in a ponytail and, even though she wore no makeup, annoyingly she still managed to look as fresh as ever (despite the fact that she had been travelling for three days straight). Zuzu had an effortless beauty I could only dream of. It was hard not to hate her, in the way that only a loving, frumpy, younger sister could do. Was it a sin to take some small pleasure in pointing out her current state of attire?

"As you well know, Jessie, my bags are coming later. And you don't prove your own innocence by proving the guilt of others. My situation is temporary. Yours is a lifestyle choice."

"Clothes are merely a necessity. I wear a dog collar. Functionality and modesty are key."

"Yes, but we found some great stuff online. Here, take my seat." Zuzu got up and pulled out the chair with a wave of her hand, indicating that I should sit down.

"I think you will find it's my seat. This is my desk. My office, remember?" I harrumphed my way to the computer. "What have you found then?"

The three fashionistas huddled behind my chair cackling over pages and pages of clerical shirts and dresses. The online offerings ranged from black jersey flared tunics with bell sleeves through to lime green tailored numbers with 'waterfall' backs (whatever they are). I admit that I was unaware that there had grown such an industry around attiring female vicars. I nodded approval and considered the possibility of purchasing a few new items — until I saw the prices.

"How much? 1600!"

"That's Swedish Krona, Jess. Not pounds. Here, let me hit the Union Jack at the top to convert the price." Sam leaned over and started to manoeuvre the mouse. "There. £133"

"For a sludge green jersey top! Please, I know you mean well but that is way out of my price range. Now, if you don't mind, I actually need to get on with some work. Barbara, there are still the last-minute preparations for my collation and the bishop's visit we need to run through. Sam? Zuzu? I don't mean to be rude but…"

Like naughty schoolgirls, my sister and best friend sulked their way to the study door before bursting into giggles and skipping off towards the kitchen.

"I'm so sorry Vicar, they were very persuasive. But, with respect, I do think they have a point. I was at a diocesan conference last year and most of the female vicars were wearing, well, a bit more colour than you do."

Barbara Graham was a fan of bright and bold fashion; her vibrant wardrobe matched her equally vibrant personality. She was a larger-than-life lady whose laughter comfortably outshone her dazzling earrings. In contrast, I am a plump church mouse in looks and temperament best suited to more sombre hues like navy, grey and black.

"Barbara, I can't afford a new wardrobe, and especially not at those prices. Anyway, I kind of broke the budget on this little number already. I have invested in a new chasuble for my Welcome Service. I just hope it gets here in time." I opened up a more traditional Polish clerical clothing website to show her a beautiful, cream, gothic chasuble and stole with an embroidered dove in white and gold thread flying downwards against a golden trinity of rings representing the Holy Spirit. "I know it's expensive, but you don't get installed in your own parish every day."

"Indeed, you don't, Vicar. That is stunning and you will look wonderful. The abbey will be full of flowers. The florist on Market Square has recommended irises for this time of year, so the abbey will be awash with blue and yellow hues. I will make sure the cleaners have polished every bit of marble and brass 'til it gleams. Bishop Marshall had better bring his sunglasses with him!" she laughed.

The Bishop of Stourchester was coming to the Isle of Wesberrey to conduct my official collation or Welcome Service. The purpose of the service was to formally hand over the benefice of the Parish to the new parish priest. During the ceremony, I am handed the keys to the church, literally handed the keys, while the local school choir and the congregation sing. I also get to ring the church bell, which I was crazily excited about. I had watched and supported in these services elsewhere but now it was my turn. My own parish. With my white gown and the abbey filled with flowers it would be like my wedding day, well the closest thing I would probably ever get to one of my own.

And like any nervous bride, as the day drew closer, I was growing more and more anxious about what could go wrong from falling over my vestments to messing up my lines. Fortunately, the words of the service and all stage directions are printed on the Welcome Service leaflet that had arrived that morning.

"Barbara, will you pretend to be Bishop Marshall and help me run my lines, please?"

"Of course, a chance to show you my favourite party trick!"

Before my eyes my effervescent secretary extended her neck, slightly bowing her head at the same time and in a sonorous tone read the bishop's opening statement in her poshest possible accent. It was like he was there in the room! Well, there, if he had a penchant for flowery blouses and flamingo-shaped earrings.

"Barbara Graham, you are a woman of exceptional talents! You bake, do impressions and are the most efficient diary organiser on the island. I am truly blessed to have you."

"We make a great team, Vicar. Now, the school choir. Mr Pixley is insisting on the less gifted singers playing their melodicas, which are marginally better than recorders I suppose."

"For the '*Veni Creator*'?" I asked, aghast at the notion of this beautiful Latin chant to the holy spirit being sung to the tooting of some badly played mouth pianos.

"No, Archdeacon Falconer will lead on that - he has the most scrumptious tenor voice. The children are singing '*This little light of mine,* '"

"And '*He's got the whole world in his hands*', that was my favourite as a child. He's got the itty-bitty baby, in his hands. The kids always love that bit. I'll be visiting the school tomorrow so will check out the melodicas then. Maybe I'll be able to persuade Mr Pixley to keep it to his guitar and a couple of triangles!"

"Or maybe the Boss could arrange for something to 'happen' to the melodicas," Barbara joked, as she pointed to the cross on the wall above my desk. "I think some divine intervention might be required."

Buffy-headed Marmosets

"**S**am apologises but she had to get back to the hospital. She is a blast! Not at all like I would expect a senior doctor to be." Zuzu had made herself a tuna sandwich and was putting the mayonnaise mix back into the fridge.

"Clinical Director, to be exact. She was always really bright, I remember she was so much cleverer than me at school, but then most people were. Better watch that sandwich, Hugo has got his beady red eyes on it."

Hugo was not a cat but a fluffy black vacuum cleaner, his electric eyes set to scan for any abandoned food he could sweep up. Hugo had adopted us when I first arrived. Before that, he had been living with the Island's famous feral cats who mostly hung around the graveyard at the back of the hospital, next to the church. He had taken to Zuzu straight away, as he had with my niece, Freya. Hugo was a little less sure of me, but then maybe he just knew it was better to keep a safe distance. I am allergic to cats after all.

"Has Freya eaten?" I took the kettle to the sink and started to refill it.

"No, not a bean! I think she is pining for her handsome Don."

"Dom! His name is Dominic. Poor thing, it's only been a day! Young love, eh? It's a pity you couldn't meet him." My sister had unexpectedly arrived on the same ferry that had taken Dominic back to university at the local city of Stourchester. "He has exams. Ah,

5

well at least they will both be back here for Easter. Erm, do you think you will still be here then?"

"Trying to get rid of me already, Jessie? That's not very Christian of you, or sisterly for that matter. Who knows?" Zuzu licked her finger and used it to pick up the remaining crumbs from her plate. "I never, ever thought either of us would ever come back here and yet here we both are."

Zuzu had been sixteen when we suddenly left the Island following our father's death. I was thirteen and our baby sister Rosina was ten. My mother vowed to never come back and over the past few weeks I had found out why. Whilst I completely understood her actions back then, there were no reasons now to stop any or all of us returning to this beautiful place, where generations of our family had lived before.

"So, my youngest daughter has been helping you move into the Vicarage." Zuzu took her empty plate to the sink and started to wash it up. "I thought this remote backwater would be the last place I would find her and yet here she is all loved up." She placed the cleaned plate on the draining board and looked thoughtfully out at the garden as she dried her hands on a tea towel. "Just so long as this infatuation doesn't interfere with her studies."

My niece was due back at university shortly, she had kindly offered to help me find my feet during her break and had, instead, found love. "Well, you would know all about that." I snorted. "Dom is a very lovely young man and Freya is ridiculously wise for her age. You could learn a lot from her."

"Pray do tell, Reverend Jessamy Ward, exactly what you mean by that?" Zuzu replied with fake indignation. We laughed. I had missed my sister.

"So, Sis, when are you going to tell me why you are here?" I pulled down the mint green cups I had inherited with the vicarage and plopped in two teabags. "I'm a good listener, part of the job description," I said, as I pointed to my dog collar.

"I just wanted to be here for my little sister's big churchy thing."

"But you were on the other side of the world! An exciting new project you said with, what was his name? Fernando? Saving fluffy-headed marmalades or something."

"Yes, buffy-headed marmosets in Brazil with Fre-der-ico. You know the little monkeys. Cute little fellas with a love of mushrooms. Very rare though. Difficult to find. Anyway, Frederico will have to look after them alone. I couldn't miss my sister's big day." Zuzu's response was not very convincing. She was hiding something, I could tell.

"So, after the service, you will be returning to Rio?" I asked.

"That all depends."

"Depends on what?"

"What adventures there are to be had here!" she replied.

Preparation, Preparation, Preparation

I had very little time to think about adventure. The Welcome Service was planned for February 1st, only three days away. The Archdeacon would be here to rehearse the day before and everything had to be ready. Looking out of the frosty kitchen window towards the graveyard, I wrapped an extra thick woolly scarf around my neck to cover my nose and mouth and braced myself for the cold air. The quickest way to the primary school was through the headstones and along Back Lane.

The Isle of Wesberrey demonstrated a real lack of imagination when naming its roads. Perhaps because it was such a small community, or maybe because there were no cars and, therefore, no need for any major highways it kept directions simple. The two other main arteries were Upper Road and Lower Road. Upper Road linking all the main civic and church buildings with the more affluent areas and Lower Road which weaved across the island connecting farmers and fishermen to the harbour and market. Back Lane ran literally around the back of the graveyard leading into School Lane on the right. There were a lot of lanes.

The 'Old School House' (which was now a trendy restaurant) was once the only building on School Lane but over recent years new houses had sprung up alongside it, each one filled with professional families from the mainland. The younger children all attended the modern primary school, 'Cliffview', and when they reached eleven, they took the ferry to study at one of the secondary schools in Oysterhaven on the other side of the crossing.

"Just sign the register there, Reverend, and I'll let Mr Pixley know you are here." A set of pink manicured nails pushed a flattened black ring binder out towards me from under a glass window in the reception desk.

"Thank you. I don't think we have met. I am Jess Ward, the new vicar at St. Bridget's."

"We all know who you are. Your uniform is a bit of a giveaway. And news of a lady vicar coming here and catching a murderer within her first two weeks on the island does make you the top gossip item on the local grapevine. I might not be the amateur detective you are, but even I could work that out."

"Well, that's where you have me at a disadvantage." I ventured as I signed in.

"Yes, well I suppose with all your crime-fighting and soul-saving you wouldn't have time to learn the name of the school's receptionist. Audrey. Audrey Matthews."

"Are you related to Stan, the owner of "Bits and Bobs' on Market Square?" I asked. It was obvious I had done something to upset Audrey, but I had no idea how or when.

"Stan is my husband. And you, Reverend Ward, are all he and my son talk about these days." The pink nails snatched back the folder. "Take a seat over there."

The reception was icy, and I don't just mean the one I received from Mrs Matthews. I sat on a battered sofa next to the radiator to warm up, but it wasn't working. The whole area felt tired and neglected. Parts of the carpet were held in place with gaffer tape and there were Blu tac oil stains on the walls where proud young artists had once hung their pictures.

"Ah, Reverend Ward, so lovely to finally meet you in person." I recognised the voice as belonging to the headmaster from the phone conversations we'd had about the upcoming service. Now I could see that the voice belonged to a tall, blond man in his mid-to-late forties wearing a cheap navy suit that would have fitted a shorter man much better.

"Mr Pixley, please, call me Jess. I am sorry it has taken me so long to visit the school, but once I am firmly installed in the parish you won't be able to keep me away!"

"No need to apologise. Please come on through to my office. Since we are on first name terms you can call me Lawrence." Without drawing a full breath, he continued, "My mother had a thing for Peter O'Toole, and *Lawrence of Arabia* was her favourite film. I think she was just a child when she saw it. Anyway, I suppose it could have been worse *Supergirl* came out the year I was born, I might have ended up being called Zoltar!" Lawrence Pixley rustled ahead, punctuating the one-sided conversation with a nervous sniff whenever he pushed his black-rimmed glasses back up his nose, which he did approximately every ten seconds.

Once we had sat down, I took advantage of a break in his monologue to raise my concern about the shabbiness of the reception area.

"Well, yes, I agree it has seen better days. The old heating system is very temperamental. I make sure the classrooms are warm. We can't have the children feeling cold, can we? Stourchester County Council doesn't have the funds, you see. And I can't afford a caretaker. We are a small island community. Not a high priority. Though, with the extra housing being built I have pressed for more money. The school roll has doubled in the past ten years."

"Perhaps we can do some fundraising in the meantime and maybe my verger, Phil Vickers, can take a look at the heating? He manages to get the Abbey's system to work. And he helps to maintain the Cliff railway."

"Oh, yes, Phil is a whizz with all things mechanical. He has tried but, well, between you and me, Jess, this school was just thrown up in the Eighties. I am not blaming Lord Somerstone, oh no, his lordship was a very generous benefactor but the firm he hired to do the work were little better than cowboys."

"Maybe we could talk to Geoffrey Somerstone then and see if he is willing to support the school again?" I suggested, desperate to find a way to help.

"I understand his lordship is gravely ill. I wouldn't want to bother him with all this." Lawrence shrugged his shoulders in resignation. "We'll just muddle along. I have a great little team here. Adversity builds character. What's a little nip in the air, eh? First world problems and all that."

"Hardly the same as a lack of internet coverage. Lawrence, leave it with me. I will go and see his daughter, Arabella. I am sure she would want to help."

"Jess, I don't think that would be a good idea." The lanky headmaster paused and looking quickly around him like a meerkat on sentry duty added in a whisper, "Her husband is Gordon Wright, of Wright Build Construction. It was his company, well his father's at the time, that built the school in the first place! I shouldn't have said anything. Please, let's change the subject. I understand from Barbara that you don't like melodicas."

Who Knows What the Day May Bring

T he morning of my 'big churchy thing' arrived with a wintery blast that covered the Isle of Wesberrey with a thin dusting of snow. The early ferry crossing had brought with it a much-anticipated package - my holy spirit chasuble, and a surprising, but very welcome, passenger - my mother. Forty-plus years after she had bundled us up for a new life on the mainland, my mother now sat in the kitchen of St. Bridget's Vicarage nursing a steaming hot cup of coffee.

"This place hasn't changed a single bit." My mother muttered into her cup. "I could swear it was the same two guys manning the cliff railway as were there forty years ago!"

With cars banned and the main modes of transport being either horse-drawn or on two wheels, the best way to get from the harbour to the vicarage is via a Victorian funicular railway that runs up the cliff face. It is currently run by my churchwardens Tom Jennings and Ernest Woodward.

"Tom and Ernest? No, they only started to volunteer on the railway after they retired a few years ago."

I was delighted my mother had decided to come back for the service. Over the past few weeks, I had learned that she had left because of a scandal involving my father, Michael

Ward, and a local woman, Violet Smith. A scandal which had led to my father falling to his death from the nearby cliffs four decades ago. Violet had died in the cottage hospital only last week.

"So, Zuzu is here as well. It will be quite the family reunion. Rosie sends her best, but she can't leave the factory. Teddy is in New York on business and Luke... well, she can't leave Luke in charge, can she? There would be no factory to go back to!"

"Mum, don't worry, I completely understand. I am so glad to have you here. This is more than I could ever have expected when I agreed to come back." My mother had been very vocal in her apprehensions about my return. She had warned me that I would be opening Pandora's box and she was right. "I am sure Zuzu and Freya will make an appearance soon, it's still a bit early for them." It was only nine-thirty.

"Well, I thought it best to get here first thing. I should probably go and see my sisters before the main event this evening. Clear the air. I wouldn't want any more family dramas. I am sure you have had your fill of those over the past few weeks." I noticed the tears in my mother's eyes as she spoke, as though she was doing her very best to hold them back.

"I'll come with you if you want?"

"No need dear, besides you have enough to be sorting out here. I'll go with Zuzu and Freya when they are ready. Keep them out of your hair." She smiled but her eyes betrayed her pain.

"Mum... I'm sorry I didn't listen to you. I'd no idea why you were so set against my return to Wesberrey. I understand now and I just want to say you did the right thing. You were very brave to leave everything behind and start again with three young girls." Speaking into a half-empty cup I mumbled, "Violet and Rachel Smith's funerals are planned for next week. We thought it fitting that mother and daughter should travel on together, under the circumstances."

My mother sipped her coffee.

"Nothing of that past remains here anymore, Mum. We can all move on." I cast an eye over to my mother and tried to gauge her reaction.

13

"Are you conducting the service?" Mum asked. "I don't mind if you are. Will Violet have an open casket? I would love to see for myself that she is really dead. I might stay for the funeral just to make sure." My mother's shoulders shook and, what I first thought was hysterical sobbing, soon became a strange maniacal laugh. "I might even drive a stake through her heart for good measure!" She flung her head backwards and glared at the ceiling above. "Or perhaps we need a silver bullet, you old dog!"

"Grandma?" My confused niece appeared at the kitchen door.

"My angel child!" Instantly my loving mother returned. She opened out her arms to welcome Freya. "I guess that is the famous Hugo."

Freya walked over to the back door and gently dropped her squirmy black bundle to the floor. Hugo promptly squeezed himself out through the cat flap and Freya returned to give my mother an extra tight hug. "Grandma, you never said you were coming. What a wonderful surprise, I'll go and wake Mum."

The two of us sat in silence.

"So, the bastard child wasn't your Dad's after all?" My mother's bitter mood had returned.

"Rachel? No, it seems she was Geoffrey Somerstone's." I walked around the kitchen table and put my arm around my mother's quivering shoulders. "Mum, it's time to forgive. Move on. I could call up to Bridewell Manor and arrange a meeting with Lord Somerstone. He is dying, Mum. He hasn't got very long left. I am sure he would want to make his peace with you before he goes."

Silence.

"Okay, but I want both of you with me. You and Zuzu. I need my girls beside me. And Cindy, she needs to be there too." Mum reached up with her right hand and gently stroked my left cheek. The tender moment stayed on pause until my sister came cluttering down the hall.

"Mummy!"

"Zuzu, my beautiful girl! Tell me all about Brazil."

Minutes later we were all gathered together eating poached eggs on toast and talking about the day ahead. The winter sun stretched her warming rays through the rear window casting an orange glow across the table where we sat. One big, happy family.

The Feast of St. Bridget

A round eleven o'clock I made my way over to the vestry to meet with members of the Wesberrey Parochial Church Council (aka St. Bridget's PCC) to run through any last-minute details for the evening's events following yesterday's rehearsal. Archdeacon Falconer had decided to stay overnight in a room above the Cat and Fiddle pub on Harbour Parade, close to the lower entrance of the Cliff Railway. The pub was owned by my verger, Phil, a silver-haired master of many trades, and the two men were deep in conversation when I entered the room.

"Barbara's in back gettin' the kettle on. We 'ave a choice of ginger or banana cake today, Vicar. Can't say I'm much of a fan of either but please don't tell 'er. Disliking one of Barbara's cakes is like insulting 'er personally."

Phil and Barbara were much more in the habit of throwing flirtatious compliments to each other than trading insults.

"Ah yes, Ms. Graham's cakes are legendary throughout the diocese. You have landed on your feet here, Reverend Ward, and no mistake. Yesterday's rehearsal went without a hitch thanks to Mr Vickers here. His Grace will be extremely impressed." As the archdeacon spoke Barbara's earlier impression of Bishop Marshall brought an enigmatic smile to my face. "See! Reverend Ward is grinning like the cat that's got the cream, she knows how very lucky she is to have you and Barbara here to support her." Peering over his round wire-rimmed spectacles he added, "And a nice, peaceful parish to boot."

"Peaceful? Well, let's hope so, not sure my old heart could take much more of the excitement of the last few weeks!" Rosemary Reynolds, the parish treasurer, was shuffling over from the vestry kitchen carrying a clinking tray of tea things.

"Here, Rosemary, let me take those off you." I took the tray from her hands and placed it down on the trestle table. "I thought your organ playing was exemplary yesterday. It was lovely to have the contrast between the formal hymns and the school choir's more folk like offerings. Mr Pixley is actually a very talented guitarist."

"Well, at least they didn't play those blasted melodicas! Well done Vicar on persuading the headmaster to leave them behind. I thought the children's voices were lovely by themselves. Always prone to overcomplicating things is Lawrence Pixley, but his heart's in the right place."

Rosemary bowed her head reverentially to the archdeacon as she passed and slowly made her way to her 'spot' at the other end of the table. Rosemary was the oldest member of the PCC and had proven herself to be a generous and wise supporter over the past few weeks. She could be frank but always sought to find the good in everyone, even those who had not treated her with the same respect. She had been Violet and Rachel Smith's next-door neighbour and was respectfully dressed in black. Rosemary had looked out for Rachel since she was a child and I imagined that Rosemary was missing her very much.

When Barbara had settled herself down and the tea and cake had been served, I decided to take advantage of the silence to invite the group to join me in a short prayer.

"May God's peace comfort those who are troubled and anxious, and may His love be firmly rooted in our hearts. On this, the feast day of our church's patron St. Bridget, as we come together to embark on a new journey, let us find the time to reflect on His blessings. May we grow each day in mind, body, and spirit. Amen."

"Thank you, Vicar. Now don't let your tea get cold." Barbara handed me a boiling cup of brown liquid that looked like it would take a fortnight to cool down. "I think it a very good omen that your collation is on the feast of St. Bridget. I bumped into your aunt Cindy in Market Square the other day and she was telling me it is also a pagan feast to mark the start of Spring." Barbara chuckled to herself as she cut into a slice of ginger cake with the side of her fork. "Spring! It must have been a lot warmer in the old days then - there'll be nothing springing through that layer of snow for a few weeks yet."

Archdeacon Falconer lay down his cup and saucer, leaned purposefully back into his chair and took a deep breath which heralded the start of a mini lecture: "Yes, well, of course, there is much religiological debate over the appropriation of pagan rites and rituals in the early church. Christmas versus Yule, is an example. The pagan feast of Imbolc also celebrated at the beginning of February, is associated with the Celtic goddess Brigid and the start of spring. It means *in the belly*, a time when sheep became pregnant, and the grass began to grow."

As he spoke, I drifted off momentarily. The past few weeks had reunited me with my aunt Cynthia, or Cindy as she preferred to be called. Cindy, like Barbara, also believed the choice of my collation date to be very auspicious. But then my aunt also believed that she could see the future and was the latest in a long line of 'godmothers' who lived on the island and protected an ancient triple goddess and her magic wells. According to my aunt, I am next up to be the 'godmother' and then I will pass the baton on to my niece, Freya. Cindy's ramblings and 'visions' were pure nonsense, of course.

"Reverend Ward, you would agree with me wouldn't you that modern ecumenical thinking demands that we embrace our shared beliefs to promote love and understanding in our diverse communities?" I wasn't a hundred percent sure what the archdeacon had just been talking about, but I thought nodding my agreement would be the safest way to go. "Excellent! It would appear that his Grace has made another wise appointment. Righty-ho, I think I had better retire to prepare for this evening's service. Phil, I think an early supper at the Cat and Fiddle will set us all up nicely. Bishop Marshall is expected on the three o'clock ferry so shall we aim to be done by 5.30? The service is at 7 pm, is that correct?"

"Indeed, it is Archdeacon. Though I doubt I'll have much room to eat after this feast. A wonderful spread as always." Phil patted his stomach and winked at Barbara who blushed like a pink lady apple.

Ecumenical matters aside, there was a lot of love in the room.

The Morning After the Night Before

T he unmistakable smell of cooked bacon wrapped its way up the vicarage stairs and tickled my nostrils awake. My body was much slower to react as my middle-aged joints made themselves very clear, that bacon or no bacon, they were in no mood to be rushed. My right hip seemed to be particularly painful, and I couldn't think what would have made it so. Rolling on to my left side I used my arms to leverage my way out of my warm bed and limped to the wardrobe to pull down my purple fleece dressing gown.

Since moving in, as Freya and now Zuzu and my mother were staying, I had made a point of getting showered and dressed before anyone in the house was up. As I hobbled towards the landing it was obvious from the animated voices below that today they had all beaten me to it.

"I thought it all went brilliantly! Aunt Jess looked great in that white gown thing. The bishop is quite a character, isn't he?"

"That voice! I didn't think anyone actually spoke like that! Dearly beloved, we are gathered here in the sight of God..." I could hear Zuzu doing a passable impersonation of Bishop Marshall from the top of the stairs; with practice, it could compete with Barbara's.

I took the stairs down one at a time and slowly shuffled towards the kitchen at the end of the hall. Heaven only knows what I had done to my hip, but Rosemary Reynolds would easily beat me in a hundred-metre dash.

"Jessie, what on earth have you done to yourself. You look like shit!"

"Susannah! Language! You are in a house of God!" Mum choked.

"Thanks, Sis! And Mum, it's fine, we aren't in church. I see you have made yourselves at home. What time is it?" I yawned as I rubbed my eyes.

"Nearly eleven, Barbara popped by and said you didn't have any appointments, so I let you rest. You must be exhausted after all that last night. It was a beautiful ceremony." My mother pushed a plate of bacon in front of me and motioned to Freya to stick on the kettle. "Do you want an egg? Will only take a few minutes."

"Yes, thank you, Mum, that would be lovely. Well, at least you seem in a brighter mood this morning!"

"I am happy because you are happy. There were so many kind things said about you last night. I was very proud. And before you say anything, I'm not crying. It seems your sister doesn't eat meat, so I was chopping some onions for her omelette."

"But you had a tuna sandwich the other day?" I looked accusingly at Zuzu.

"Fish isn't meat. I'm a pescatarian," she snapped back.

"Fish have feelings too."

"Is that why you collect all those hideous glass ones then, there are boxes and boxes of them in the next room. What on earth do you plan to do with them all?"

"I suggested the shed," piped in Freya.

"They are Murano glass and, as I was telling your daughter, I am going to fix up some cabinets, the ones with the built-in lights to display them properly." I had been collecting the fish for years. There is always one at every church jumble sale or bazaar. It is incredible how quickly they mount up.

"Well, it's good to see there is some colour in your life, and in your wardrobe. That dressing gown?"

"I thought you wanted me to brighten it up a bit."

"Yes, but wow, that is very... what would you even call that colour? Magenta?"

"Girls! Stop it!"

"Yes, Mother," my sister and I answered in unison.

We all laughed.

"Now, I promised your aunt Pamela, that we would all head to hers for afternoon tea. It seems that the Reverend Jess Ward has been too busy to visit the old house. Cindy will be there too." Mum walked over to my seat with the hot frying pan. "We need to join hands at the Well to seek your protection from the Goddess," she quickly added, as she slipped the egg onto my plate.

"To whom the what now?" I choked on my bacon.

"Jess, just humour us. Okay? There's no bloodletting or anything. No calling to the four winds. It's not 'Charmed'. We will just join hands around the Well and say a little prayer. That's all."

"Mum, this isn't a matter of 'just humouring' anyone. I am a fully paid-up member of the Church of England. Licensed to preach. The collar isn't just a fashion choice you know. Last night I was put in charge of the souls of the people on this island. I can't be chanting pagan verses around an ancient water hole at the bottom of some old garden."

"Then we'll go without you. Pamela will be so upset after you have spent so much time with Cindy." Mum cast me a look that always made me feel guilty, even when I knew I hadn't done anything wrong. "Just come for tea, we can take it from there. No one will make you do anything you don't want to."

"Promise?"

"I promise."

"Ooh, so exciting!" Freya jumped up from her chair, removed the elastic hairband that had been holding her copper locks off her freckled face and giggled "I'll just nip into the shower then. Promise to save you some hot water!"

"Hmm, that's perked her up. Maybe it will stop her thinking about —" But before my sister could say his name, we could hear Freya talking to Dominic on her phone as she ran up the stairs. "Or maybe not."

"Leave them alone, Sis. They make a beautiful couple. Mum, do you actually believe this family 'godmother' thing?" I had never really heard my mother talk about any of this before, though, honestly, I don't remember my mother talking about *anything* to do with Wesberrey. She rarely spoke about my father, except to say she missed him, and it was a tragic accident. She never mentioned my grandparents, my father was an only child, or her own family much. My aunts had visited us on the mainland from time to time. "I mean if Cindy is right then after me comes Freya. And that means she won't have any children of her own. That's not fair."

My mother slowly pushed back her chair and started to collect up the empty dishes.

"It doesn't mean she can't find love," she said.

Thinking about my aunt Cindy and myself, childless and alone, I found my mother's words cold comfort. Not that I believed any of it, of course.

Ding, Dong, Dell

Pink and green, pink and green, pink and green. Aunt Pamela's lounge looked like a Laura Ashley design set from the Eighties. A flowery green wallpaper strip divided the room into two shades of pink: dark below, and light above. Botanical prints lay trapped beneath pale pink card borders in gilt-edged picture frames. Floral sofas with matching floral cushions screamed to their floral curtain neighbours. I felt my hay fever taking hold just entering the room, though there wasn't a real pollinating bloom in sight.

"Byron is working in his shed. We shouldn't be disturbed." Pamela sat down on a green damask wing back chair and motioned for us to join her on the floral sofas. "We will just wait for Cynthia. She always *was* tardy, wasn't she, Beverley? Even as a child, always kept us waiting." My mother nodded in agreement.

The pendulum of the mahogany wall clock marked out each second, its ticking tock the only sound - bar the occasional shuffling of awkwardness as we sat and waited. A faint whirring warned of the approaching Westminster chimes. It was four o'clock.

On cue, Cindy appeared at the patio doors. As always, her silver hair was perfectly wrapped into a smooth raised bun and was held magically in place with a lilac chiffon scarf.

Finally seeing the three sisters together after all these years, their physical similarities and distinct differences were mesmerizing. They were undeniably related. They shared a mellow look around the eyes I had never really noticed before. They were of similar height and build and each one had maintained their trim figures. (That gene had obviously passed me by). It was as if they were a set of dress-up dolls, each sporting a different hairstyle and outfit. If you swapped their wigs and clothes over, they would become each other. Cynthia was like the moon, light, ethereal. Pamela, a sturdy tree, earthlier and more fixed. My mother, Beverley, a furnace, both a source of warmth and potential danger.

Familial pleasantries exchanged, the sisterhood moved to the kitchen where they started to collect a few 'essentials' for the trip to the Well in the back garden.

"Byron and I made the dolls last night." Pamela pulled out a wicker basket from under the sink and emptied the contents onto her pine table. "Byron has moved the chimenea closer to the Well so that can act as a hearth and keep us warm."

"Corn dollies?" I asked, picking up one of six straw figures dressed in skirts of white cloth and fresh leaves.

"Yes, they are actually called Brideog - a traditional gift at Imbolc. We'll each take them back to our homes to bring new hope for the Spring." Strangely, it never occurred to me that all three sisters would take part in these ceremonies. I thought only Cindy was the mad new-age hippy but as I watched them busying themselves with the preparations, I realised that this had been a major part of my mother's world too. It was as if they had gathered to cook the Christmas dinner.

Cindy took some small pieces of paper from the basket and handed them around. My mother followed behind with a selection of colour pencils.

"Pick the colour that speaks to you and write down your hopes for the coming year. Then roll them up and keep them with you as we head out into the garden." When my mother got to me, she stopped. "Jess, it's just a prayer."

"You promised me no calling on the four winds and all that nonsense," I replied, but dutifully took the pencil.

We walked in pairs to the well at the corner of Pamela's garden, each carrying a Brideog, our rolled papers and a white tealight candle.

"Isn't uncle Byron joining us?" asked Freya.

Cindy smiled and leading Freya by the hand explained that this was a ladies only celebration. When we reached the well, Cindy continued to explain the meaning of Imbolc and the legend of Brigid, Goddess of fire, blacksmiths, wells, healing waters, springs, and poets. She is also linked to motherhood, fertility, and abundance. She is a busy goddess.

"Please everyone, place your gifts along the edge of the sacred well and join hands."

Cindy proceeded to pull out a bundle of sage from one pocket and a gold lighter from the other. She lit the sage and walked around our backs waving the smoking herb in the air. The garden now smelled like a roast dinner.

"Sage is to help cleanse and purify the air as we work," my mother whispered.

As the sage burnt down Cindy threw the remaining leaves into the well and then passed the lighter to Pamela who used it to light her candle before passing it on to my mother who did the same and so on until all six candles were lit.

The cold night drew in quickly and soon we were only able to see each other by the light of those candles and the warm glow of the chimenea in the corner.

"Please sisters, take your rolls of paper and use your candle to set them alight, then throw them into the well." We all did as instructed. "Very good. Now, let's hold hands. In your own mind remember the words you wrote down, feel a wave of energy fill your heart as we call upon our Earth Mother. She is coming to bring us new hope for the year ahead as she clears away the darkness of winter and brings in the light of spring. Repeat after me..."

This was the bit I had been dreading, writing a few words down on a bit of paper in coloured pencil and holding hands was fine, but incantations to an earth goddess? What would Bishop Marshall say if he knew?

Cindy continued:

"Although it is now dark, we come seeking light.

In the chill of winter, we come seeking life.

We call upon the fire, that melts the snow and warms the hearth.

We call upon the Sun, that brings the light and warms the earth.

Like fire, light and love inside us will always glow.

Like love, wisdom, and inspiration inside us will always grow.

Fire of the hearth, blaze of the sun, cover us in your shining light."

"Amen." I added, "Sorry, force of habit."

I looked around at my family gathered in the twilight moon. Their faces glowing in the light of the candles and chimenea. A warm loving feeling filled my breast. I looked to the heavens awaiting the thunderbolt from on high, but it didn't come.

Pamela rubbed her woollen gloved hands together. "Right-y-o, who wants a cup of cocoa?"

"With marshmallows?" Freya asked.

"With marshmallows. I managed to get some gelatine free ones from the market earlier in the week. You are vegetarian aren't you, Susannah?"

"Pescatarian, but thank you, Aunt Pam, that sounds wonderful!"

I stood back and watched as my aunts, mother, sister, and niece linked arms and strode back into the distant glow of the French doors that lead inside the house. It's just a harmless family tradition that's all, I said to myself as I followed in behind them. I am sure my 'Boss' would understand.

I took a last look into the well and wondered how deep it was. It seemed terribly dangerous to have an open well in your back garden, but then my cousin was a grown man and he and his family were living in Australia now so no threat to grandchildren running around. I picked up a small stone, leant over, threw it in and waited. It was several seconds before the splash.

"Death is coming to Bridewell!"

27

"What? Who said that?"

I looked around expecting to see my aunts or sister but there was no one there.

"Byron?" maybe he had left his shed at last.

"Freya? Is that you? Are you messing around?"

Silence, except for the odd crackle from the chimenea.

I realised I was feeling a little lightheaded. "Jess, hearing voices now, are you?" I mumbled to myself as I headed towards the house. "All this calling on the goddess nonsense is starting to make you a little crazy. You just need some food and a warming cup of that cocoa."

Mr Peasbody

"**S**o, you just held hands, lit some candles, and said a few words. Sounds like the stuff you do every Sunday."

I had popped in to see Sam at the Cottage Hospital before my morning rounds.

"That's not the point," I protested. "We were chanting and calling in the power of the Earth Goddess. I am a vicar!"

"Well, I hope so, you are conducting a double funeral tomorrow! Is your mother staying on afterwards?"

I shrugged my shoulders. "I guess it'll all depend on how dinner at Bridewell Manor goes." When Lord Somerstone heard that my mother had returned for my welcome service, he sent his butler around with a gilt-edged invitation for this evening. "Cindy is joining us. Mum is pleased about that, strength in numbers I suppose. Zuzu and Freya are so excited to see inside the gothic mansion. Mum is really anxious though. It's been forty years!"

I was a little anxious about the '*Death is coming to Bridewell*' thing as well but I wasn't about to share such nonsense with Sam.

"I am sure she will be okay. She is a very strong woman. Talking of Lord Somerstone, it is good of Lord S to allow Violet and Rachel Smith to be laid to rest in his family's mausoleum. I suppose it is fitting as Rachel was his daughter. Leo was doing all the preparations yesterday."

"Leo?" I asked, detecting a sight blush to my friend's cheek when she mentioned his name.

"Yes, Leo Peasbody. The undertaker from Oysterhaven. Peasbody and Sons always do all the Island funerals." Sam said this with a wry smile.

"So, tell me more about this *Leo* Peasbody?" I leaned onto her desk and rested my chin on both hands, elbows together, eyes wide open in anticipation.

"There is really nothing to tell. We just, well, it started out purely professional you understand. They store the recently deceased here in the hospital. We have a small mortuary in the basement. Leo does all the necessary stuff, embalming and so on. If they are being buried on the mainland or cremated, he takes them back in his horse-drawn hearse on the morning ferry. Otherwise, he stays here with the corpse until the funeral."

"He sleeps with the bodies?"

"No! He sleeps at the Cat and Fiddle, well he used to."

"He used to?" I probed. Sam was squirming a little in her chair and was looking a tad flushed. This was going to be interesting I could tell.

"Well, that seemed an expensive option so one night I suggested he could stay with me at the cottage and well..." Sam blushed.

"Well? Don't hold out on me now!"

"He sleeps in the spare room."

"Don't believe you! Is he married or something?" I asked.

"No!"

"So, what's the problem? Tell me."

"But you're a vicar!"

"And your best friend."

"Take off the dog collar and I'll tell you."

"Don't be ridiculous!"

"Take it off or I won't tell you about Leo."

I unbuttoned my collar hoping again that my 'Boss' was otherwise engaged for a few minutes.

"Thank you. You must promise not to say a word when you meet with him later." Sam moved in closer and peered at me over her designer frames. I nodded. "Leo Peasbody is, how should I describe our arrangement? A friend with benefits. He saves himself the cost of a room and treats me to dinner at the Old School House instead. Then we snuggle up together for extra warmth."

I coughed. "Erm, I've seen the prices at the Old School House. A night at the pub would be cheaper!"

"Yes, but then he wouldn't get to spend the night with me! You are enjoying this aren't you?"

"Immensely." I gestured at her to carry on. I needed to know more details.

"Leo is very tall, about six-three, six-four. Taller than me, which is essential and difficult to find around here. He's a widower. He has three children. They all work in the family firm. His eldest two sons will be here for the funeral. Good looking lads. He has slightly horsey features I suppose but they suit him. Blond with flecks of grey. Very distinguished in his long coat with that touch of velvet on the collar."

"So, two questions. How long has this been going on and why didn't you tell me before? Has he been staying with you this past week?" I suddenly realised that my best friend, who had been an almost daily visitor (usually bearing a bottle of something left by a grateful patient), had not been around as much this past week. Unless you count that time I found her with my sister criticising my wardrobe choices.

"That's actually three questions! Two years, because you're a vicar and yes."

"Two years!" Sam glared a 'don't judge me' look back across the desk. I relaxed into my chair. "I'm not shocked, honest. So, are we talking a potential husband number three?"

Sam laughed and pushed herself off from the desk, her chair gliding back on its castors towards the filing cabinets behind. "Now, who's being ridiculous. We are just friends."

"With benefits?" I replied.

"With benefits." Sam smiled. "Oh, before I forget. I bought you a little something. I saw them in town and thought we could have a pair each." She shuffled her chair forward and opened a drawer to the right of her desk. She pulled out two black velvet jewellery boxes, raised their lids and placed them in front of her. Grinning, she turned them both around to face me. Inside each box was a pair of identical gold circle stud earrings with faceted dark blue stones. "They're lapis lazuli. They represent friendship, openness, and honesty." She pushed one box towards me.

I carefully picked it up. They were exquisite.

"You got these in Market Square? From a stall?"

"Yes. She told me she only made these two and no one has shown any interest before so won't be making any more. I thought they would help me make amends for attacking your fashion sense the other day. I can't make fun of you if we are wearing the same thing."

"They are stunning!" I said, taking out my plain gold studs and replacing them with my new pair. "I will wear them every day. No more secrets. Openness and honesty, right?"

"Jess, I promise. No more secrets."

Burying the Hatchet

"**S**o, who was that long streak of gorgeousness I saw you with in the church?"

My sister had a keen eye for a handsome man.

"That was Leo Peasbody, the undertaker. He was running through the arrangements for Violet and Rachel's entombment. The service is slightly different from a burial, logistics-wise."

Zuzu and I were bringing up the rear of our mini caravan to Bridewell Manor. Cindy and Freya were way out in front, my niece buoyed on by my aunt's tales of the film stars and musicians that visited Bridewell in the later sixties and early seventies. I had discovered, since my arrival a few weeks before, that my aunt had been a frequent visitor to the Manor during those hedonistic years, and it was the scene for some crazy happenings. My mother was walking by herself. I felt guilty for falling back and leaving her alone with thoughts of my father and the alternate lifestyle he had indulged in with his best friend, Lord Geoffrey. My father had been a frequent visitor to the big white house and had taken a full and active part in its peculiar leisure activities right up to his death, despite being a married man and father of three. This journey back into the past was going to be hard for her.

It had been my mother's idea to walk the twenty minutes or so along Upper Road, from the vicarage to Bridewell Manor, notwithstanding the weather and all of us being in our best clothes. My aunt, sister and niece were each carrying tote bags with a change of shoes in addition to the small hand torches we all held for additional safety on the road. It was a clear night, but the waning crescent moon provided little light. Though there are no cars on Wesberrey and therefore traffic is limited to the odd scooter, bicycle, or horse-drawn cart. The last hundred yards or so along the cliff edge could be precarious at night, even with modern barriers and solar powered lanterns illuminating the pathway. I had to hand it to the residents of Wesberrey for finding a sustainable yet modern way to light up the roads. The main junctions had electric streetlamps, but solar energy was being fully embraced elsewhere. If we weren't heading to such an awkward meeting this would have been a very pleasant evening stroll in the country.

"Zuzu, did you know about our father's nocturnal adventures up at the Manor with Lord Somerstone?" I whispered.

"Nocturnal adventures! Jessie, you do have a funny way with words! Well, there was gossip at school, but I didn't believe any of it. Or I chose not to... I mean, I was only sixteen. I thought they were just being cruel." Zuzu hung her head as she talked. "Then he had the accident and Mummy bundled us all off to that awful hotel in Stourchester. I didn't even have time to say goodbye to my boyfriend. I cried for days. Can't even remember his name now."

"So, you don't remember him at all?" I asked.

"His kisses tasted like a stale ashtray, put me off smokers for life."

"I was talking about Dad, not your boyfriend. Zuzu, you are unbelievable!" I shoved my sister playfully.

"What are you two fighting about now? Good grief, as if this wasn't bloody painful enough! Just grow up, the pair of you!" My mother was obviously tense.

"Sorry, Mother," we answered in unison.

At the top of a slight incline sits a bench placed to take full advantage of the views over the water to the mainland. The last time I was there I had had an interesting conversation with Hugh Burton, a rakishly handsome film and small screen actor enjoying a renewed period of fame through a popular television series entitled 'Above Stairs'. Though I had never watched it I am told it is quite a raunchy tale of life in Edwardian England. Hugh was also enjoying a long-term clandestine relationship with former actress Arabella Stone, daughter of Lord Geoffrey Somerstone, heir to his vast estate and wife to business magnate Gordon Wright. Hugh had been staying at the manor in secret. I wondered if he was still there.

The next turn brought us to the wrought iron gates that locked us out, of course, they also locked the inhabitants of Bridewell Manor in. As we passed through the security of the gatehouse the pebbled pathway sliced through the snowdrifts that still clung to the edges of the lawn from the flurry we had earlier in the week. Everywhere else on the island the snow had melted quite quickly but here at the highest point with minimal traffic it remained. The result was a spooky monochrome landscape that took full advantage of the leafless trees and the imposing white turreted building ahead.

Death is coming to Bridewell. I shook my head, as if that would help shake out the nonsense, though the winter scene ahead made the perfect setting for a gothic crime.

Freya slid back down the path, obviously excited to be joining the aristocracy for dinner.

"It's like the set of a Tim Burton movie! I expect 'Jack Skellington' to pop out from behind a tree and throw pumpkins at us." she giggled. "Aunt Cindy has been telling me all about when the Rolling Stones partied there and other actors and actresses, I have never heard of but didn't want to let on. I can't help being so young. But Terence Stamp sounds a great character, I will have to look up his films when we get back. It's a shame Dominic isn't here. He would love to paint this. Stop everyone! I want to take a photo."

"Nonsense, it's too dark. C'mon, let's get inside." My mother was impatient to have the whole ordeal over and done with. Softening she added, "Angel child, you can come back up in the morning and take a picture when it's light."

"Of course, Grandma." Freya kissed my mother warmly on the cheek and linked arms. They both found new energy and, united in love, marched confidently up the remaining few yards to the large black wooden door in front.

***

"Reverend Ward! How wonderful to see you again. I am so sorry none of us were able to attend your Welcome Service, Papa has been so ill these last few days. I have been at his bedside all the time."

Arabella Stone appeared to have walked straight out from the pages of Vogue magazine. There was no denying she has a charismatic presence and eternal beauty that transcended the long-term damage the much-documented drug abuse of her youth has wrought on her face. She was wearing a soft black velvet ankle-length tube dress overlaid with a sheer petrol blue netting-like material. I am no fashion journalist so have no idea how to describe it except to note that it was figure-hugging and the effect was stunning.

"Arabella, we are all extremely honoured to be invited." I shook her elegantly extended hand. "Please allow me to introduce you to my mother, Beverley Ward."

Polite introductions were made, and Arabella called on her butler to take us through to a cloakroom to the side of the marble hallway to hang our coats, change shoes and so on. I looked at my weather-beaten reflection in the cloakroom mirror and caught sight of my mother applying a slither of red lipstick. She smiled back, took a deep breath and sighed.

"Right, let's do this!"

Cindy pulled my mother towards her and blew gently on her face. It seemed to calm her.

"Remember this. Michael loved you above all others. You are beautiful."

"And alone." My mother replied.

"We are all alone."

"And beautiful!" Zuzu pulled us all together to face the mirror. "Look at us! I'm guessing that was an Armani, his Autumn/Winter collection is all black and blue velvet this year. It must have cost a fortune. But just look at us, eh? Stunners the lot of us and not a designer gown in sight."

"How would you know about Armani's winter collection from the jungles of Brazil?" I laughed.

"They have designer shops in Rio, you fashion philistine. One of my favourite spots was the Avenida Ataulfo de Paiva in Leblon, let's just say Frederico has a healthy credit card balance." Zuzu explained as we emerged back into the hallway.

"And will the results of these shopping trips be following on with the rest of your luggage?"

"Probably. I do hope the food is as good as her fashion sense, I'm starving!" And with that Zuzu flashed me a brilliantly white smile and lead the way into the dining room.

The whole of Bridewell Manor had been modelled on the Gothic Revival style of the Strawberry Hill House, once owned by Horace Walpole. In the late eighteenth century, the first Earl of Stourchester, wanting a house befitting his new title rebuilt the earlier Elizabethan manor house into the imposing fairy-tale castle it is today. The dining room was a magnificent addition. Gold-leafed cherubim and seraphim looked down on us from their vantage points on the highly carved vaulted ceiling, and light from the moon outside shone through the arched windows that ran along the full right-hand side of the room. In the middle stood a long oak table carefully set with white porcelain, gold-edged crystal glasses and candlesticks. To our left, a large stone open fire was lit. At the head of the table, in a wheelchair with attendant IV drip stand and connecting tubes, sat Lord Geoffrey Somerstone.

"Welcome, my dears! I have set a place for you at my right, Beverley. And Cindy, please take a seat to my left. So many beautiful ladies. Please join us."

"Reverend Ward, please will you sit beside me. Allow me to introduce you to my husband, Gordon Wright. Gordon was in London on business when you first called. And these are his business associates. I hope you don't mind them joining us for dinner tonight, their arrival this afternoon was a bit of a surprise. But there is plenty of food and wine for all. It has been a long time since we have entertained a full party. It's wonderful to bring a bit of life back to the old place."

I cast a quick glance at my mother, grateful for the mixed company that, hopefully, would relieve some of the pressure she was clearly feeling about getting through dinner. She seemed at ease, perhaps finally seeing Geoffrey Somerstone in such an obviously fragile state helped to soften her mood. My aunt Cindy, in contrast, appeared quite shocked by his appearance, but then they had once been lovers. My sister was wasting no time in getting herself introduced to Gordon's business associates, whatever had actually happened in Rio with Frederico was clearly now a distant memory. Freya was taking photos of the impressive architecture on her phone.

I had not met Gordon before, but Hugh Burton had described him to me as a 'toad of a man' which I had put down to jealous rivalry, but Hugh's description was spot on. It was hard to see him married to the glamourous Arabella.

"So, Reverend Ward. I am so sorry to have missed Bishop Marshall, but business kept me on the mainland. His son boards with Tris." Tristan Somerstone-Wright was the couple's only child and went to a private school on the mainland. "Bella has been filling me in on all the gory happenings though. You really are quite the hero, I understand. Such heroic derring-dos are great publicity for the Island. We will soon have lots of mystery hounds flocking here to see the detective vicar! Great for business. This house would be a magnet for ghost hunters and murder mystery fans." Gordon stuffed a prawn into his mouth and continued. "I was saying, Eric - this priest murder mystery thing is great for business, eh?"

Eric nodded. Eric was one of Gordon's mysterious business associates. Eric appeared to be a man of few words but did look like he spent considerable time in the gym.

"Eric, what line of business are you in?" I asked.

Wiping his mouth with his hand, he looked at me thoughtfully, eventually answering.

"Customer relations."

"Ah, very nice. So, you all work in the city then. Do you still run your father's construction business, Gordon?"

"I am on the executive board, but father made sure I would never need to lay a single brick. Not sure Bella would have married me if I had workman's hands. Bella prefers pretty boys, don't you, my love." I noticed Arabella blush and wondered again if Hugh Burton was hiding somewhere. As the conversation progressed, I learned that Gordon's return was as unexpected as the visit of his associates. It was very possible that Hugh was squirrelled away in secret cupboard in the west wing.

After we had eaten a glorious main course of monkfish, Arabella suggested that I walked with her to the kitchen. Under the guise of informing cook that we were ready for the next course we made our excuses to the rest of the party and went to the servant's quarters downstairs.

"Reverend, I am so sorry, but I needed to get you away. I have a favour to ask you. I know you must think me a terrible harlot, but you see ..." Arabella's tubular gown appeared to be working overtime to keep her from falling over, released from enforced politeness she seemed to physically fade in front of me. "Gordon only married me for the estate and my title. We did our duty, produced the heir and then we have really gone our own ways. I thought he would have the decency to stay away until Papa died and then he turns up out of the blue announcing that he has invited some people to stay and that they would be here for dinner tonight."

Arabella paused. Her eyes pleading with me to understand what she was trying to say.

"Where is Mr Burton?"

"Hugh is hiding out in the barn on the edge of the farm. Though I suspect my micro pigs are better company tonight than those Neanderthals."

"I think you are being unkind. Eric seems pleasant enough."

"They are thugs in suits. What on earth is Gordon doing having any business with them! I see your sister was flirting with the one with the gold necklace, Tony, I think his name is. You should warn her that tan isn't the only fake thing about him."

"Arabella, is Hugh safe out there, it's going to be a very cold night?"

"That's why I wanted to speak to you, Reverend Ward. May I ask a favour?"

I nodded and urged her to continue.

"I need to help him get away. Gordon is watching me like a hawk, and he keeps sending Ralph on stupid errands when he needs to help with Papa."

"Ralph?"

"Papa's butler. I need him to stay in the house. Ralph is devoted to my father. This evening is important, Papa is so happy to entertain his old friend's family at his table again."

I refrained from adding anything about that family being driven away because of her Papa's entertainments. This was a night for reconciliation.

"I am not sure how I can help?" I said.

"Hugh was to return for filming in a couple of days anyway, he just needs somewhere safe to stay." Arabella tilted her head and looked at me.

My shocked hands quickly covered the words that rushed from my mouth. "You want me to hide him at the Vicarage!"

"Or in the church, think of it as a form of sanctuary?"

"Arabella, I'm not sure. I mean —"

"I will pay for the church roof to be fixed, it needs fixing, doesn't it? They always do."

It was pitiful to see the desperation in Arabella's face, whatever I thought about her affair with Hugh, and her sham of a marriage, it was clear that she loved the actor greatly.

"Okay, two nights max. There's a servant's attic, I haven't been up there yet, so cannot say what state it is in, but it will be safe and warm, maybe there is still a bed there. Call him and tell him to head there straight away. I never lock the front door. I probably should, but —"

"Thank you, thank you, thank you!" Arabella threw her arms around me and hugged me so close her tears soon soaked through the shoulder of my blouse. "I'll call him straight away. Can you let Cook know we are ready for dessert?" Her hand dived into the top of her dress and produced an ultra-slim phone which she immediately began tapping with her perfectly manicured fingers. I carried on down the corridor towards the brightly lit room ahead and found Ralph the butler in a tender embrace with the cook. It was all going on tonight.

"Excuse me, Reverend, but my wife Annie here was getting a bit stressed out by all this unexpected catering. I was telling her that you all enjoyed the monkfish."

Annie wiped her tears on the back of her sleeve and bobbed.

"Sorry Ma'am, it's just what with His Lordship being so ill for so long we've hardly had to prepare any meals for ages and now, all of a sudden, I am feeding the five thousand!"

"Annie, you have done splendidly. Is that dessert?" I said eyeing up a series of beautifully decorated glass bowls. "Ralph, I think we are ready for you to bring them through."

I walked slowly back to the dining room, meeting a restored Arabella on the way and we calmly sat back down discussing the amazing design of the chandeliers in the hallway as if nothing else had happened. I was really hoping that my 'Boss' was having the night off, I was not sure if he would approve of all this subterfuge.

Secrets and Lies

"Right, who wants some cocoa? I think it's going to snow tonight." My mother was biting off her woollen gloves and kicking off her shoes as she spoke. The rest of us followed in behind her. We had taken one of the Island's horse-drawn taxis home and the ride had been frosty in more ways than one. No one had said a word all journey.

"Beverley, we need to talk." Cindy hung up her coat and followed her sister down to the kitchen.

I went to join them, but Zuzu held me back.

"Give them some time. Why don't we go into the morning room? I believe there's still some of Sam's whiskey in there. We haven't had a proper grown-up drink since I got here. Freya, do you want to join us?"

"Mum, erm, if you don't mind, I need to speak to Dom, he wants to know everything about the big house. I could come down later?"

Zuzu smiled and with a nod of her head granted my niece permission to disappear to her room, which Freya took immediate advantage off, leaping up the hall stairs two at a time. As Zuzu and I turned to enter the morning room, Freya screamed!

"Hugh! Sugar, I forgot!"

Freya almost fell down the stairs to escape the dark man with bewildered blue eyes standing by the top banister, innocently holding a familiar black cat.

"He's got Hugo!" she gasped.

"I'm so frightfully sorry if I caused alarm. I was looking for a way to get into the attic and this little thing kept getting between my legs. I think he is hungry."

Regaining her composure, Freya took a deep breath and walked slowly back up the bottom steps. "Just give me the cat. Nice and gently."

"Oh, of course. Is he yours? Beautiful feline specimen. Reverend, I must apologise for the inconvenience. Please, may I come down?"

"Hugh, of course. Please accept my apologies. I should have told my family you would be here. Zuzu, Freya, this is Hugh Burton. Arabella's friend. He will be staying here for a few days." Hugh walked down and handed his latest conquest over to my niece, who turned on the spot and marched the purring bundle straight out into the kitchen. "Hugh, I believe my mother has put the kettle on, please join us. "

***

My mother appeared to enjoy having a handsome guest to fuss over. On learning that he had spent the day in the pig shed she set about opening tins and pulling out the contents of the fridge to create a warming meal for the Bridewell refugee. As she beavered away at the stove, Hugh regaled us all with his story about how Gordon has returned home unexpectedly and in a foul mood. Hugh had to make a quick dash to the pig shed leaving most of his clothes and his dignity behind.

"Arabella stole away as soon as she could to bring me some blankets and what-have-you. It was perishing cold in that shed. I thought to myself, Hugh ole boy, this is it. This is how you meet your maker, eaten alive by a ravenous pack of bloody micro-pigs. Oh, the ignominy!"

Freya still viewed Hugh with deep suspicion, glaring at him from across the kitchen table. Cindy and Zuzu, however, were enraptured, each of them leaning in closer and closer with every word.

Zuzu finally came out of her trance. "Jessie, you were going to make this poor soul skulk about in the attic. Not very Christian of you."

"I wasn't thinking very clearly. I was kind of ambushed. Anyway, where else was he going to sleep? I knew Cindy was staying the night."

"He can sleep my room," Zuzu replied.

"Zuzu! Have you no shame!" My mother slammed down some cutlery on the table.

"Not with me in it! Sheeeeesh, what you think I am? I can bunk in with Freya. Can't I, Frey-Frey? it will be like when you were little."

Freya harrumphed a response.

"Mr Burton, you need to get off this island on the first ferry out in the morning." Cindy stood up and walked around the table. She took Hugh's hand in hers and turning it palm side up, traced her long middle finger along its lines. "I understand you don't want to leave her. You are frightened for her, but she will be okay. It is your future we have to protect now. Things are going to get a bit difficult over the next few days and you need to be as far away as possible."

"But my train ticket is for the day after tomorrow. I have first-class reservations. This face cannot travel economy." Hugh protested. Crouching down Cindy placed her hand over his and fixed him with her gaze. He nodded. "I understand. I will leave in the morning. But I need one of you to warn Arabella. Those men who were at dinner tonight. They aren't Gordon's friends."

"Whatever do you mean?" I asked. I was also wondering what on earth my crazy aunt was talking about. *Death is coming to Bridewell.*

"I overheard them talking when I was in the shed. They were outside having a smoke. Arabella hates cigarettes, especially around her sick father. From what I could hear, the Toad has been trying to swindle them with some fraudulent investment scheme. They are not the kind of gentlemen to take kindly to such trickery. It seems they have offered him a chance to make amends, so to speak. He, in turn, has offered them, Bridewell Manor."

"But it isn't his. Is that why they were at dinner tonight?" My head was spinning. Was Arabella in danger, from her own husband?

"In a way. Bridewell will be Arabella's once her father dies. This was an opportunity to show them around the house and for them to see how close to the end Lord Somerstone is. Poor man. They are like a pack of hyenas waiting to pounce." Hugh shook his head. "I know the old fool hates me, but no one deserves to be treated like this."

"He doesn't have much longer, a week at best." Cindy stroked Hugh's hair as she rose and patting him gently on the head added. "You and Ms. Stone will be together soon. Have faith. Love is very strong. It triumphs in the end."

There was my aunt doing all her fortune-telling nonsense again. Last time I had had to reprimand her for scaring Freya with warnings that my life was in danger, though admittedly she had been right, that one time. Cindy was simply saying what Hugh needed to hear I told myself. It was a comfort to him. I bit my tongue. I would pick this up with her another time.

"I don't understand," said Zuzu, "If Bridewell will be Arabella's how can those guys benefit from it?"

"Because Gordon is going to turn it into a hotel. And the hotel will be a front for their other business activities."

"What? Money laundering?" My mother gasped.

"I believe that is the terminology, yes. Mrs Ward, we cannot allow this to happen."

Hugh turned to my mother. Their eyes both knowing the bitter tears of separation caused by the actions of Geoffrey Somerstone. Hugh had stood by and watched the love of his life marry an odious man because her father willed it and my mother had lost her husband as a direct consequence of being a partner to his best friend's reprehensible life. I was sure they both resented the man who had caused them both so much pain but at that moment they were united in an altruistic desire to protect his legacy.

Smiling, my mother spoke. "You get the ferry, Mr Burton, I will warn Arabella. You have my word. Now, eat. You need to keep your strength up."

Outgoing Tides

F reya announced over breakfast the next morning that it was time for her to return to university. She had already packed her bags and would catch the ferry with Hugh Burton. She joked that she was returning because she wanted some peace and quiet, but I feared she was going to find university life a bit staid after all the recent happenings here on Wesberrey.

After an early morning feast of my Mum's incredible ham and mushroom omelettes, (I have repeatedly tried but failed to replicate these gastronomic masterpieces) our extended party made its way down to the ferry port. The funicular railway cabin allegedly holds eight people but the six of us just barely squeezed ourselves in, and Freya was the only one with any luggage.

Ernest Woodward was in solemn attendance at the Cliff View end of the line; his partner Tom Jennings, in contrast, cheerily waited at the harbour end.

"Ooh Mr Burton, what an honour. I was wondering when we would have the pleasure of your company on the Cliff Railway. If it's not too much of an imposition, I was wondering, may I have your autograph? You are simply splendid in 'Above Stairs', though, of course, I can remember you from your earlier films. Television acting doesn't have the stigma it once did, does it? I imagine it pays well these days too. And you still get to make love to all those ingénues. Hmm, I see you haven't tried to fight the ageing process. Embrace the laughter lines, that's what I say."

"Er, yes of course. You were a fan of my films, eh? Any particular favourite?" Tom had magically produced a small notepad from a drawer under the ticket booth and a pen. He passed it to Hugh. "To whom should I address it?"

"Tom, Tom Jennings." Hugh duly signed the notepad and returned it to my beaming churchwarden. "And I wouldn't say any of them were my favourite. They were all pretty awful, weren't they? You're doing a much better job now."

Wanting to avoid more avid autograph hunters, Hugh pushed the hood of his tracksuit top up over his trademark floppy black hair and pulled out a pair of ladies' sunglasses from Arabella's hastily packed hold-all.

"If I'm lucky," he mumbled, "people will think I'm just a pretty ugly woman."

"Darling, here," Cindy took off her baby pink neck scarf, "wrap this around your neck. Every actor needs the right props."

Freya marched ahead, her ginger locks running away from the oversized rucksack that crawled up her back.

"Can we please get a move on? If we miss this one, we will be stuck here for another hour!"

The mid-morning sun played with the waves as seagulls dived in to pick up the rotting fish parts left by last night's fishing trawls. They found slim pickings as the Island's feral cat colony had been here from sunrise and had already had a mighty feast. This breakfast of kings would sustain them on their leisurely amble back up to the church graveyard, where they would await their supper of tinned rabbit. I wondered how Hugo would react to Freya's departure. He had made firm friends with my niece, but at least he would find my sister a good companion, for as long as she planned to stay.

Hugh Burton slipped quietly on board the ferry, pausing briefly to pay his fare to the ferryman Bob McGuire. Bob screwed up his face in a way that suggested he knew the face under the sunglasses was familiar but was one, fortunately, he could not place. Freya's farewell, in contrast, was a chorus of emotion. To facilitate the great escape I had had to cancel my morning meeting with Barbara. As a result, Phil and Barbara were at the quayside to bid my niece goodbye.

"You'll need some tray bakes to keep you going on your journey up north, my dear." Barbara squeezed a small Tupperware container filled with what looked like chocolate brownies into Freya's rucksack. "Our loss is archaeology's gain."

"Anthropology." Freya smiled graciously at my parish secretary "I'll be back at Easter for a few days, it's only a couple of months away. This place is hard to resist."

"And, Frey-Frey, I'll look after Hugo for you." My sister possessively pushed her way through to hug her daughter goodbye. "I will probably still be here when you return. If that's okay with you Jessie?"

"Mi casa es su casa," I replied.

"You are a sweetie. Oh, look! Isn't that Tony and what's his name from last night? With the Toad man. Looks like they are going into the Cat and Fiddle."

Phil glanced over to his pub and started walking backwards with a dramatic wave.

"Duty calls, ladies. 'Ave a safe trip!"

As we watched the ferry chug its way around the headland my mother cast us all a mischievous look.

"I don't know about all of you, but I rather fancy a pub lunch."

What Lies Ahead

O ur impromptu meal had produced very little in the way of further intrigue, much
to my mother's disappointment. Gordon Wright and his 'friends' Tony and Eric
had secured a table in one of the pub's cosiest nooks and it was impossible to hear any
of their conversation. Tony had left them at one point to take a call on his mobile phone
which appeared to make him agitated, but he soon regained his equilibrium over a plate
of the Cat and Fiddle's legendary lamb shank.

Talk on our table turned to more pecuniary matters.

"So, Cindy, how much do you know about this trust fund Geoffrey was talking about last
night?"

"Darling sister, I know as little as you. I haven't properly spoken to Geoffrey for years, not
since...well since Michael's funeral."

"Trust fund?" Zuzu's ears had an impressive way of responding to tales of financial gain,
much like her eyes were quick to respond to a handsome male face.

I had no choice but to tell my family what little I knew.

"When I first met Lord Somerstone, he said that he had created a trust fund for the three
of us using the uncashed cheques he sent Mum after Dad's death. He said that he had

been assured by you, Aunt Cindy, that the three of us would return to Wesberrey one day."

"And by the 'three of us' you mean, you, me and Rosie?" Zuzu looked confused.

"Yes. I asked Ernest about it. There was also one set up for Rachel Smith."

"Ernest?" Zuzu rubbed her forehead and sat further forward on her chair.

"Ernest Woodward, my churchwarden. You met him this morning at the top of the Cliff Railway."

"Okay, now I'm totally lost! Why did you ask the guy in the ticket office?"

"Because he is a solicitor. He acted for the Somerstone Estate before entering semi-retirement. It doesn't really matter. He wouldn't tell me how much either fund was worth. Ours will only be released upon the death of Lord S and only if all three of us have come back to the Island. Poor Rachel died without knowing a thing about her inheritance." Which reminded me, I had a double funeral and entombment the next day I had to prepare for.

"Mummy, we need to get Rosie here pronto! There could be a small, or even a large, fortune with our names on it ready to drop at any moment!" Zuzu clapped her hands with excitement. "Jessie, pray tell me why you haven't bothered to mention this before?"

"Because it's blood money and we want nothing to do with it!"

My mother slammed down the tumbler glass she had just been holding to her now trembling lips. Her eyes rimmed with water ready to overflow the banks of her reddish-brown lashes. Cindy reached out her slender hand to her sister and squeezed her arm.

"The money will be theirs. It is their right. It will be a blessing to them all."

"There is nothing good about taking anything from that family. Cindy, are you sure?" My sobbing mother explored my aunt's face, looking for comfort.

"I am sure, Beverley. In a week Geoffrey will pass and your darling Rosina will need somewhere to make a fresh start. Everything is as it should be, my dear."

Cindy nudged her chair across to my mother and wrapped her weeping sister in her arms.

Zuzu and I looked at each other. I relaxed a bit. Of course, Lord Somerstone is close to death, no mystery about death coming to Bridewell there. And then I realised what else my aunt had said.

"Aunt Cindy, what's going to happen to Rosie?"

May They Rest in Peace

T he early twentieth century Willis organ flooded St Bridget's Abbey with Mozart's *'Ave Verum Corpus'*. The tragic double funeral service for Violet and Rachel Smith had begun.

Maybe agreeing to Rosemary playing the organ at such an emotional event was possibly not the best idea. A difficult piece for even the most accomplished player. I suspected that the many bum notes probably had an emotional cause. After all, Rosemary had been like a mother to Rachel and had tried her best to be a good neighbour to Violet.

Looking down at the gathered congregation from the altar, I could see from my mother's face that she was enjoying the messy recital a little too much.

Arabella Stone sat in the opposite pew looking elegantly aloof from the rest of the congregation. For all her riches, she cast a lonely figure. Obviously, her father was too ill to attend, and Hugh had left the day before, but I was surprised to not see Gordon by her side, especially given his impending new role as lord of the manor. It would have been an excellent opportunity to ingratiate himself with the local community.

I was pleased to see that Sam was wearing her new earrings, clearly visible as her hair was snatched up in a practical ponytail. Following her blushing gaze, my eyes easily found the long, dark figures of Leo Peasbody and his two sons solemnly standing to the side. All three dressed in black wool long coats with discreet velvet collar trims. Each respectfully holding in their hands a silk top hat with black mourning veil. Looking back down the aisle I observed that these three handsome men had found another admirer, namely my sister Zuzu. I really do not know where she finds her constant enthusiasm for fresh blood.

The floral offerings were beautiful if a little sparse. There were a few sheaths and cushions arrangements from members of the parish council and some of the other traders on Market Square. They were all for Rachel. A white and green cross and a card sat on top of each coffin, these it turned out were from Lord Somerstone. Violet's card read *'To my raven-haired muse.'* Rachel's simply read *'For my daughter.'*

After the ceremony, Leo Peasbody slowly led the possession through the church to the graveyard at the rear of the vicarage. The small congregation followed with his two sons acting as lead pallbearers. Phil, Stan Matthews, Bob McGuire, Tom, and Ernest carried Rachel's coffin with great dignity. A mixture of volunteers from the parish helped with Violet's. As there was a rather precarious walk to the Somerstone Family mausoleum, the coffins were transferred to wheel biers outside the church and the pallbearers were given some relief. At the mouth of the tomb, they were enlisted again to help transfer the coffins onto specialist lifting platforms inside the crypt. The platforms raised Violet and her daughter up into their marble resting places, to sleep together side by side for all eternity.

I entreated those gathered to join me in a final prayer whilst Leo's sons sealed everything up. I will admit that it was a huge relief. Everything had gone smoothly, no one caused a scene, and no one dropped a coffin. The whole ceremony had, in fact, been quite moving. As the mourners snaked their way back through the headstones to the vestry for refreshments, I spotted the willowy outlines of Sam and Leo walking in the opposite direction. They appeared to be deep in conversation. I wasn't being nosy, just curious. My eyes followed them across the graveyard to the grounds of the hospital. The thought that they were off to find some 'alone' time at such an occasion was rather shocking, maybe this was a business meeting?

"Reverend! Should I save you a sandwich?" the shrill voice of the parish secretary cut through the quiet air, disturbing my slightly envious musings. It has been many years since I had sneaked off with a handsome man.

"Thank you, Barbara. I will be along in a minute."

Looking back to the main body of mourners I noticed that the peculiar party of my mother, Cindy, Zuzu, and Arabella had splintered off towards the Vicarage. I truly hoped that the funeral of her nemesis would give my mother much-needed peace. Beverley Ward was, without doubt, the strongest, most giving person I knew. She would instinctively offer her time and money to anyone in need, but boy could she hold a grudge if you betrayed her. She was very unforgiving to anyone who hurt her or her family. It was difficult to reconcile this harder side of my mother with the image of the passive stay at home wife who accepted her husband's multiple and varied infidelities but that was the reality of my childhood, though I was unaware of it at the time. I suppose I owe that ignorance to my mother. She had protected us then and was keen to protect all the innocents again now.

As I entered the sacristy to get changed, Ernest Woodward was waiting by the entrance.

"Reverend Ward, I was hoping to speak to you alone. We need to talk. It's about Violet Smith's will!"

Expect the Unexpected

"**E**rnest, please take a seat." I ushered my churchwarden into the sacristy as I carefully removed my vestments. "How can I help you?"

Ernest linked his gloved hands together and took a deep breath.

"I need to inform you, Reverend, that you and your sisters have been named joint beneficiaries in Violet Smith's will."

The shock almost made me blaspheme. Almost.

"I'm sorry, Ernest, can you say that again?"

"Of course," he cleared his throat. "Violet Smith identified that the beneficiaries of her estate should be her daughter Rachel and her siblings. Or, as she defined them, all living children of her beloved Michael Ward."

"That is crazy. It cannot be legal?" I sat down on the sacristy chair with a discernible thud. "What if Rachel had lived, surely she did not mean for her daughter to have to share her inheritance with us? This is madness. Rachel was not my sister!"

"I am afraid that the document was drawn up by my partner at the time. I took over his accounts when he died. The will is over thirty years old, and Violet testified to being of sound mind and body. To my knowledge, it was never superseded and stands. I assure you, Reverend, I was unaware of its contents when we last spoke."

It was a good thing that the chair was so solid, or I would have literally sunk through the floor. I looked up at Ernest who was walking slowly towards me with an outstretched arm. I took his hand, and he helped me to stand.

"I need to tell my family. What would happen if we refuse the bequest?"

"Reverend, you can, of course, give the proceeds of the estate to a charitable cause and I would understand that decision. The estate could yield a significant revenue with the sale of the house and the book shop. I will leave you to talk to your sisters and we can meet in a few days to talk about how to execute the instructions."

Ernest left to join the other members of the PCC in the vestry where undoubtedly Rosemary would be reminiscing about Rachel and walking her to school as a child and bemoaning Violet's ingratitude. Barbara and Phil would be trading playful compliments over a slice of alcohol-soaked fruit cake and Tom would be telling everyone about his encounter with the famous Hollywood actor and ageing gracefully. I knew I needed to put my most professional foot forward but as I caught my reflection in the sacristy mirror my eyes gave truth to my total confusion and exhaustion. This was going to be hard and, as I adjusted my dog collar, I prayed that the 'Boss' was not looking the other way this time. I really needed his help.

Fancy Bumping Into You

Two days and numerous heated conversations had passed since Ernest's revelations about the contents of Violet Smith's will. Having set off the incendiary device when I had returned to the vicarage, I admit that I tried to avoid the debates that followed. Zuzu was enraptured by the idea of a double inheritance windfall and had secretly been on the phone to my younger sister, Rosie, begging her to come to Wesberrey the moment her husband Teddy got back from the States. And at times I thought my mother was going to march up to the Somerstone Family tomb and rip Violet out of her marble bed. It was, therefore, a huge relief whenever I found work that required me to leave the vicarage and on today's list was a visit to a sickly parishioner in his cottage on the far side of the island.

The snow flurries of a week ago were now a distant memory and, for an early February morn, the air had an almost tropical feel. I took an island taxi across to the most easterly tip of the island, a bleak yet intoxicating landscape of sand dunes and low-level scrub vegetation. It is a popular destination for wintering bird populations. Historically the same river systems whose grinding waves had brought down the shifting sand deposits from the mainland had also brought with them a rich variety of fish. The combination of cold and saltwater species living in abundance within an easy day's sail of this area had led to a booming fishing trade. Whilst a few men continued to venture out each day from the ever-changing banks, most had abandoned the quaint fisherman's cottages that edged the pathways to live closer to the larger boats that set sail from the main harbour.

"The next ride back into Market Square passes this point at noon today, Vicar. Miss that and you'll be here past teatime. One of our drivers has called in sick, you see."

"I will bear that in mind. Thank you." I carefully stepped down from the carriage and handed the driver my fare. Cash is king if you want to navigate your way around Wesberrey without your own transport, but it's not very convenient or sustainable in the long term. My aunt Cindy had lent Freya and Dominic her old Vespa scooter a few weeks before, perhaps I should invest in a motorised set of wheels for myself.

The fisherman's hut I was heading for had been described to me by Barbara as 'slightly off to the left after the junction, whitewashed stone, a low wall outside, blue door.' Seems that the family name of 'Spillett' would be above the entrance. Not much use for Google maps here. A row of white cottages crept onto the horizon as I reached the junction and within a few minutes I was knocking on the Spillett's sea-weathered door. Mr Joshua Spillett was a very stubborn old seafarer who refused to leave his family home for hospice care. His wife, clearly also in her mid to late eighties, fussed around his chair which was pressed close to the window so that her life-long partner could watch the incoming tide. I said a few words of comfort and we prayed. There was very little else I could do. I hoped my visit brought some comfort to this ailing old man and his loving spouse. I promised to return again in a couple of days and began to walk slowly back up to the main road.

As I stood at the taxi stop, I noticed what looked like a line of black ants marching in the distance, except they were walking alongside each other not following each other as ants are wont to do. The line drew closer and closer and then I heard the clear sound of dogs barking. With each step, the line appeared more animated.

"Spread out! We need to cover this area before dark!"

I knew that voice.

"Inspector! I think I have found something!" The line broke up and a central group of black dots shifted to where the second voice had come from. There was a huddle and the black shapes fell, rose again and then dispersed.

"False alarm! Keep looking." It was *his* voice.

Inspector? It was, I knew it. It was Inspector Dave Lovington. My heart sped up. What was he doing back on Wesberrey so soon and why was there a search party on the dunes?

Be Still My Beating Heart

T he search party edged closer to the main road. With every step, my heart rate
increased. I had foolishly developed a bit of schoolgirl crush on the lovely inspector, with his ridiculous pencil moustache, amber-brown eyes, and slicked-back hair.
On anyone else, the cliché detective look would be laughable, but on him, everything
sat perfectly. I had briefly entertained the idea that he had been flirting back with his
continuous winking, but I now suspected he had a nervous twitch. I last saw Inspector
Dave Lovington when he took my statement at the hospital and to be honest, with so
much going on, I had rarely given his full lips and square jawline much thought, most
days.

However, the Inspector was now easily within calling distance. Surely it would be the
professional and courteous thing to do to get his attention and offer assistance. There
would be absolutely nothing inappropriate about that. After all, I am here on official
business, if anything he is on my turf. This is my parish. Maybe a parishioner's dog is
missing? Oh my! The thought occurred to me that it could be a child! No time for silliness.
I had to offer help.

A neighing horse broke me out of my thoughts. The taxi had arrived. I mentally slapped
myself across the face and reluctantly climbed aboard.

"Market Square then Vicar, hold on tight! Wilberforce here had few too many oats for breakfast. Apologies in advance for any unusual smells on the wind."

"Market Square will be perfect, thank you. I don't suppose you know what the police are searching for in the dunes. Looks like quite the operation."

"Ooh, haven't you heard. Missing person. That poncy bloke that lives up at the Manor. Married old Arabella Stone. What's his name?"

"Gordon Wright!"

"Yes, that's him. Been missing a few days. They reckon he's done himself in. I was talking to Bob at the ferry earlier and it seems the police were asking him if the missing chap had taken a ferry to the mainland. Bob was clear he hadn't. He was last seen at the Cat and Fiddle. Having lunch, he was, with some business types."

Death is coming to Bridewell.

"And no one has seen him since, not even his wife?" I asked, remembering that Arabella had been alone at the funeral. Was Gordon missing then? Was he still alive?

"I heard it was her what reported him going AWOL."

"And his business associates, are they missing too? Maybe they took a boat out or..."

"Nah, what I heard is that they have already spoken to the police. After their meal, they bid Mr Wright farewell and jumped on board the next ferry. Bob confirmed it."

Well, as I have learnt, Bob knows everything about the comings and goings on Wesberrey so that must be true.

"It's a large police presence for one man."

"That it is, Vicar, but money talks don't it. No shortage of overtime when something happens to one of the establishment, eh?"

"So, Gordon Wright has been missing for four days."

My interest was piqued. If Tony and Eric had left on the next ferry, then that didn't necessarily cut them out of whatever had happened to Gordon. If indeed anything had happened to him. It only meant that whatever happened didn't happen immediately after the meal because they were on the ferry. They could have circled back later on a private boat. Or maybe he went to join them. Perhaps he sneaked onto a later ferry in disguise as Hugh had done. The real question was why?

Arabella was alone at the funeral but didn't appear to be in any way concerned about Gordon's absence. Did she know then he was missing? Surely, she would have mentioned it. My mother said that Arabella was shocked by the revelation that her husband and his business associates had unethical designs on her family home.

Maybe she had confronted him later that day. They had a fight. He stormed out and Arabella told the police he went missing the day before, to protect herself. But why do that unless she knew what had happened to him and needed an alibi? And that didn't explain why he wasn't at the funeral in the first place. Did Arabella know already about her husband's plans and pretended to be shocked when my mother told her? She was an actress, maybe the whole thing was a performance for our benefit and Gordon had already gone. Or perhaps he was dead! Was Arabella a murderer? Surely not. Though I had suspected her before.

Wow, what a crazy imagination I had developed! Gordon had probably had a little too much to drink, wandered home, got himself lost and was holed up in a barn somewhere sleeping it off. For four days? Maybe, he had slipped on the icy road and fallen into a ditch or something. I was sure he would be found alive and slightly embarrassed. The voice from the well kept circling around my head. I needed to get a serious grip on myself.

The taxi carriage pulled into Market Square, and I decided that what I needed was some afternoon tea, and perhaps a little gossip, in the Cat and Fiddle before venturing back home.

Everything Stops for Tea

"So, when were you going to tell me about Hugh Burton staying at the Vicarage? Jess, don't deny it, Cynthia told me all about it. She said Tom managed to get an autograph, but I don't suppose for one second any of you thought to get him to sign anything for me! I was telling Byron wasn't I, my dear." My aunt Pamela looked to her husband for confirmation. He duly nodded in the affirmative. "I was telling Byron I am always left out of the family adventures. Even after inviting you all to celebrate Imbolc in my home and doing all the preparation." Pamela swallowed her words as she looked down into her lap. She paused, obviously contemplating whether she should carry on. After a wary glance over her shoulders, she added in a frustrated whisper. "I didn't get an invite to Bridewell Manor. Oh no. Even though I am the eldest sister. I inherited the house with the Well. I should have been the 'godmother'. I should be the head of the family. But no. Cynthia is the wild one, the beautiful one, the gifted one. The one invited to glamorous parties. And now this!" Pamela placed her hands on the edge of the pub table to steady herself as she spoke. "You have my favourite actor sleeping under your roof and not one of you thinks to call me."

"Aunt, believe me, I had no idea!"

Pamela and Byron had bumped into me on the corner of Market Square, so I had politely asked them to join me for something to eat in the pub. A decision I was starting to regret a little.

"I suppose Cynthia told you I never leave the house, that I don't want to miss my programmes." Her eyes locked me in their sad gaze. "But no one ever asks me. They just assume. Beverley is only back here five minutes and Byron, you wouldn't have minded me having a night out with my sisters, would you dear?" Byron slipped the remaining edge of an egg and cress sandwich into his mouth and shook his head.

"Aunt Pamela, I think Mum wanted us there for moral support and took Aunt Cindy because, well, she and Lord Somerstone had a relationship in the past. I am sure she wasn't deliberately excluding you. As to Hugh Burton, his stay was totally unexpected. I didn't know he was your favourite actor. I am sure he will be back one day. Cindy said as much."

"Did she? Well, he will then. Just remember, I am his biggest fan. Now, Jess, do you want the last sandwich?"

"No, thank you. Please, be my guest." Pamela placed the last sandwich on her husband's plate and cut it in two, taking one half for herself.

Cindy had assured Hugh that he and Arabella would be together. Did she foresee Gordon's disappearance? Surely not. The timing of her 'premonition' was eerie though I had to admit. "Would anyone like some more tea?"

After her tirade about not being invited out to Bridewell Manor and associated adventures, my aunt's conversation turned mainly to catching me up on the latest happenings on 'Above Stairs'. Despite my repeated protestations that I had never watched it and knew nothing about the characters she spoke of. Over a second pot of tea and an exceedingly light scone with strawberry jam and a wicked amount of double cream, I learnt about Hugh's character, the exiled Duke of Belrovia. How he had been a bit of a cad in his youth but was now a reformed man thanks to the love of a good woman. That 'good woman' was Mabel Stubbs, the daughter of a textile baron from Bradford and some twenty years his junior. The duke, it seems, wasn't Mabel's only suitor. Captain Davenport who, Pamela was certain, would face a tragic end in the trenches of World War I in the next season, had insulted Mabel's honour at a ball held in the grand house. And the last episode of season four had seen the Duke and the Captain squaring off in a duel.

"It looked like Davenport had engaged the first shot as the credits rolled, but if Hugh Burton was heading back to film season five, he must survive, right?"

"I imagine so, Aunt. It all sounds so exciting. I will make a point of watching when it returns on TV. Now, I am sorry, but I need to run a few more errands before heading back home. You both stay here and finish up. I will just settle our bill at the bar. It's been lovely spending some quality time with you."

I backed away towards the bar.

"Reverend Ward?"

I knew that voice. I turned around carefully, telling myself not to 'spin' around and appear too excited.

"Inspector Lovington! What a surprise. I heard you were back on Wesberrey. Something to do with the disappearance of Gordon Wright. Will you be staying here in the Cat and Fiddle?"

I could feel my cheeks flush.

"Yes, I will be. In fact, it is rather timely to see you here. I was going to pop in to speak with you later. I understand from Mr Wright's wife, Arabella, that you were all at a dinner party the night before he disappeared."

"We were, Inspector, and I also saw him in here the following day."

"Well, then, you may have lots of useful information. Do you have time to join me for something to eat now? You can share your thoughts over one of Phil's specials."

I wanted to kick myself for declaring to my aunt and uncle that I had important places to be. I would have happily forced another plate of sandwiches, even a four-course meal down me if it meant staring into Dave Lovington's golden-flecked eyes for an hour. All as part of my civic duty to help find one of my parishioners, you understand. However, I had to make my apologies.

"I will come up to the Vicarage later then. Who else was with you?"

"Cindy. My niece Freya, but I am afraid she has left to return to university. My mother Beverley and sister Zuzu." The Inspector wrote down all our names in his black notepad.

"Thank you, Reverend. I will need to speak with you all." Inspector Lovington stared at his notepad; his handsome brow furrowed in the most appealing way. There is something very attractive about an intelligent man in the process of deep thought. "On second thoughts, Reverend, rather than my coming to the Vicarage would you be willing to all come down here to give witness statements? Around midday tomorrow. PC Taylor will be able to help me. Unless Mr Wright turns up by then, of course. I might manage to pop into Cynthia's cottage later."

"No problem at all, Inspector. I could ask Cindy to join us. Save you the trouble of visiting her today. You must be very tired after all that searching you were doing up on the dunes."

"How did you know we were on the dunes today?" A quizzical look knitted his perfectly smooth eyebrows together.

"Erm, I saw you in the distance and the taxi driver told me you were all out looking for Gordon. I was visiting one of the old fishermen."

"Ah, right. I thought for a second you had psychic powers."

I laughed.

"No, I leave all that mumbo jumbo to my aunt Cindy."

The Inspector took a step towards me, leaned in and whispered in my ear.

"That's a shame. Cynthia has a really extraordinary gift."

Closing his notebook with a snap, he grinned, bowed, and walked off towards the bar to get his room keys.

Does my aunt have a gift? I remembered that she said she had helped the Inspector before. Did she use her 'gift' to solve a crime? He seemed keen to go to visit her. Maybe he thinks she can 'see' where Gordon is. Why does everyone buy into all this nonsense, even an intelligent, cosmopolitan man like the Inspector? I let those thoughts swirl around my head as I walked across Market Square. I also swirled around the memory of how warm Dave's breath had been on my earlobe. A strange thing to fixate upon but the recollection made me feel a little fuzzy all over. I couldn't help but smile.

Careless Whispers

"You look cheerful this afternoon, Vicar! Great to see you out and about after all the drama. Have to say that was some adventure, chasing down a murderer. Not the usual sort of thing on Wesberrey. You're the talk of the town, as they say."

"Yes, Stan. I understood as much from your wife, Audrey. She didn't seem too impressed with my heroics, though."

"My Audrey? Aw, don't pay her no never mind. She's just miffed she missed all the excitement. My missus hates to feel left out. So, Vicar, what can I do for you? Adopted any more of our feral friends?"

Stan, the sanguine owner of the local hardware store 'Bits and Bobs' was in a buoyant mood. When we first met, I had obviously disturbed him during his breakfast, most of which was dribbling down his vest. Today, his rotund figure was wrapped in an intriguing dark brown tee-shirt with a picture of Chewbacca at the centre. It was a large image that placed the Star Wars furry warrior's mouth directly over its wearer's belly button. Not a great look, but at least it was clean. As with most island residents, I had only met Stan a couple of times, but we appeared to have bonded over the dramatic capture of Rachel Smith's murderer.

"No, Hugo is enough cat for me. I just need some nails to hang up a few pictures around the vicarage. Make it feel more homely."

"No problem, Vicar." He lifted a heavy wooden flap in the shop counter and walked to the back of the shop where a range of screws, nails and other fixings were hung up in small plastic wallets from protruding metal arms. "Terrible news about Mr Wright though eh, Vicar? My Audrey says good riddance. She was shocked at the way he spoke to Mr Pixley the other day. S'pose money doesn't buy you class. That'll be £2.99. Anything else I can help you with?"

I shifted slightly to my left to allow Stan to get back to his till.

"No Stan, that'll be all. So, Gordon Wright was up at the school! I wonder what all that was about?"

"Haven't the foggiest. To be honest, Vicar, when the missus talks about work, I tend to zone out a little. Only took interest cos' she said Pixley got into a bit of a scuffle. Something to do with the heating, I think. But Pixley playing fisticuffs, I would have paid to see that. That man couldn't rip a tissue!"

"So, Audrey says that Lawrence Pixley and Gordon Wright had a fight!" I was shocked. Though I agreed with Stan's summation that Lawrence wasn't the aggressive type I could imagine him being drawn if his beloved school was under threat. "Has she spoken to the police?"

"Nah, why? You don't think Lawrence Pixley had anything to do with Wright's disappearance, do you?" Stan suddenly became even more animated. The idea of helping to solve another mystery was obviously very attractive.

"Of course not, but I think Audrey should talk to the Inspector. He is in the Cat and Fiddle right now, I just left him. I could easily pop back on my way home and tell him."

"Would you, Vicar. I will call Audrey. She'll be so excited!"

And with that, he disappeared behind the brown curtain at the back of the shop and I marched back across the Square, obviously keen to fulfil my civic duty.

Cold as Ice

My return visit to the pub was brief and uneventful. The Inspector thanked me for my time and politely dismissed me with a wave as he called PC Taylor on his mobile phone. How I had ever imagined that our relationship was anything other than professional now perplexed me in the extreme. There is a saying that goes 'there is no fool like an old fool' and I really *was* beginning to feel my age.

I entered the vicarage to the sound of raised voices coming from the kitchen. My mother and sister were fiercely debating the contents of Violet's will, again, so I tiptoed my way through to the study. It had been a long day and the last thing I needed was to get embroiled in another row over the morality of taking over Violet Smith's house and shop. Even from beyond the grave her obsession with my father was in danger of destroying my family.

Time for something completely different. I logged onto my ancient computer, its spinning wheel of determination letting me know that it was trying really hard to connect me to the internet, to a saner world of cat videos and online shopping. Cabinets for my glass fish, that was on my list for today. Everything else had been unpacked and they needed a bright new home.

Several minutes later I was happily using the zoom feature to explore different lighting options when I heard a small tap on the study window. Probably the wind, a wayward branch perhaps. Then again, louder, clearer. It had gone five o'clock and outside was already dark. Another tap, more of a rap this time. And a cough. I distinctly heard a cough and a sniff. I slowly got up from my desk and walked over to the box sash window behind me. Under the window stood a sideboard with a green angle-poised lamp to the side. I grabbed the lamp and pointed it at the window. The light revealed a dazed blond man with a handkerchief raised to his mouth.

It was Lawrence Pixley.

I mouthed to him to go around to the front door where I met him and quietly guided him into the study. The man was frozen.

"Reverend, I'm so sorry to disturb you. I've just had a visit from the police. They heard I had a small exchange with Gordon Wright the other day and, oh heavens, sorry. They think I might have been the last person to see him alive! That makes me a suspect! Me!"

Lawrence sat awkwardly on the wing back chair by the study's fireplace, his long legs struggling to find a happy home. The monogrammed handkerchief that usually flagged attention to his constant sniffing was now being wrung out like a dishcloth in his nervous hands.

"Lawrence, you are freezing. Let me get you a warm drink. Perhaps something to eat as well? A bowl of soup?"

"Tea would be lovely, thank you, Reverend."

"Please, call me Jess. I will be right back. Just stay here and warm yourself by the fire."

I knelt down and switched on two bars on the small electric fire that sat where once a beautiful hearth had stood. They buzzed into life. First a neon pink then orange glow. Cleaner and more efficient this may be but the next thing on my to-do list would be to reinstate the coal fire. This particular fire was probably older than me.

"What were you thinking, coming across the graveyard without a coat? Hope you are feeling a little better now." Lawrence cradled the hot cup with his long fingers and sniffed a weary smile in response. "Now, why don't you tell me all about your encounter with Gordon Wright."

"Well, I think it was on Tuesday, the fourth, wasn't it? I am afraid my memory isn't all that for such details. The Inspector was most determined to get a date out of me. I am sure it was the Tuesday, but it could have been before or after. All I know for sure is that it was in the afternoon at about 3.45 pm. The children go home around 3.30 pm and very few hang around in the winter. It gets too dark going home you see."

"I understand. If it helps, Violet and Rachel's funeral was on Wednesday. In fact, I also saw Mr Wright on Tuesday at lunchtime, so it is very possible he walked up to the school shortly afterwards. Pray continue."

"Mrs Matthews was in the back of the reception office and I was in the main foyer. I was changing the strip light in the ceiling. I wasn't expecting him to pop in so soon you see. I had thought about our conversation and well, rather than bother Lord Somerstone or his daughter, I had contacted Wright Build Construction direct. The secretary there must have called Gordon Wright. I didn't even know he was on Wesberry."

"And there was no one else around? None of the other teachers?"

"No, they were all in their classrooms tidying up or preparing for the next day. Anyway, he started off friendly enough, though he did seem a little vexed now I come to think about it. But I took it to just be his manner. Some people are just tetchy all the time without any good reason, aren't they? He promised that soon he would be in a position to support the school more."

"Okay. But I understand that Mrs Matthews believed that you were involved in a scuffle. How did that happen?"

"Did you speak to Audrey?" Lawrence's demeanour changed. His body became taller and more rigid.

"Actually, I spoke to her husband."

"So, it was you who told the police? Why would you do that? I wouldn't hurt anyone." Lawrence jolted out of the chair, dropping the half-drunk cup of tea on the stone hearth with a loud crash. Like a frantic house spider emerging from the protection of its ball, his long limbs scrambled towards the hallway.

"Lawrence, please, I don't think you had anything to do with Gordon's disappearance. I only thought it would help the police create a correct timeline. Please sit back down. I'll get you a new cup of tea."

"No, thank you, Reverend. As you said I need to go and get my coat. No need to let me out."

Lawrence pulled open the door and pushed past my mother and sister who had rushed from the kitchen to investigate the sound of breaking china.

"Is that the headmaster?" my mother asked, her eyes following his escape around the side of the vicarage as she closed the front door.

"Jessie, no wonder you don't have a boyfriend if you keep chasing away all the men on the Island." Zuzu laughed. "I will go fetch the dustpan and brush."

I stood in the middle of the room totally perplexed at what had just taken place. Was Lawrence scared of being a suspect in Gordon's disappearance because he is a generally anxious person, or did he know something about what had happened? He never got around to telling me why he and Gordon had fought. He was definitely afraid of something. I tried to run the conversation back in my mind. Walking it through I noticed he had left something behind.

"Poor guy, the visit from the police must have really spooked him. He even dropped his handkerchief and now it's covered in tea. I will wash it and hand it back to him at Mass on Sunday. And apologise, of course. Maybe he will open up a bit more once he has calmed down."

I looked up to see my mother and sister standing side by side shaking their heads at me in perfect unison.

"Jessie, promise us you will leave the investigations to the police this time. Gordon Wright is probably just waiting out Geoffrey's death somewhere away from all the drama at Bridewell Manor. How do we know he is even missing? What, because Bob McWhat's-his-name is certain he didn't leave on the ferry! That wretched Gordon man has a lot on his mind. Not easy work planning to turn your wife's family home into a den of thieves. I would stay away too if I were him. He probably has no idea anyone is even looking for him."

"But, Zuzu, if I can help? By the way, Inspector Lovington would like us all to give statements tomorrow. I said we would go down around noon. Do a bit of shopping, grab a pub lunch?"

"Will that family ever give us any peace?" my mother muttered, as she turned back down the hall.

Inspector Lush

The door to the makeshift incident room at the Cat and Fiddle opened slightly to reveal my sister standing disturbingly close to Inspector Lovington. It was not my imagination. Zuzu was clearly flirting with the Inspector. Her breasts visibly heaving, she bit her bottom lip and flicked the edge of his business card off the index finger of her left hand. Then the giggle. And finally, the flick of her hair as she waved goodbye. I forced myself to look for his reaction. Sadly, he seemed to have enjoyed the show.

"Your turn, Jessie. Boy, you didn't mention how totally lush Inspector Dave is. I fear that dog collar has cut off all your senses." Zuzu flopped casually onto the banquette seat beside me and made a play of fanning herself with his business card.

"Oh, take a cold shower!" I whispered, as I tried to compose myself. I could feel the tears pressing the back of my eyes. Naturally, someone like the Inspector would fall for my sister's charms. Like attracts like. What foolishness to think anything different. I had a job to do, a serious one at that. Just give my statement and then we can eat.

"Ah, Reverend Ward. Please take a seat. I just had the most interesting conversation with your younger sister."

"Older. She's three years older than me."

"Really? My mistake. Anyway, both your mother and sister's statements mention a certain famous visitor you had over after your dinner party date up at the Manor. Would you care to elaborate further?"

"Oh, they both told you about Hugh! I am not sure what I can add, Inspector. Hugh was staying with Arabella. Gordon turned up unexpectedly and Hugh needed a place to stay. He left the next morning."

"Yes, with your niece, Freya. Is that correct?"

"Well, technically, yes. But they were travelling separately. Freya didn't like Hugh that much."

"I see. And may I ask, Reverend Ward exactly when you were going to share with me Gordon Wright's plans to turn Bridewell Manor into a hotel? Or Hugh Burton's claims that Mr Wright's business associates were planning to use the hotel as a front for their other businesses?"

All of the petty, jealous thoughts I had been harbouring about my sister and the Inspector were suddenly replaced by ones of shame and embarrassment.

"You do realise, Reverend Ward, that withholding evidence pertinent to an ongoing police investigation is a very serious matter."

I couldn't make eye contact. I felt suitably chagrined.

"I am really sorry, Inspector. I really don't know why I didn't mention it before. I mean I realise now that these events might be connected to Gordon's disappearance. Well, if I'm honest I knew it immediately when I heard about Gordon from the taxi driver but... it must have just slipped my mind."

"Slipped your mind? How, exactly? Please Reverend, I am all ears."

Now was not the time to admit I forgot because I was too busy contemplating the touch of his lips on the back of my neck. I was such a fool! I looked up sheepishly at the Inspector, who had laid down his pen and pad, his arms folded across his chest. I tried to speak but found my mouth too dry.

"Were you trying to cover for Hugh Burton? You were quick enough to point the finger at Lawrence Pixley. But then I suppose he isn't a handsome movie star. I am disappointed, Jess. I thought you had more substance than that."

"What? Are you trying to suggest I have some stupid crush on the Duke of Belrovia?

"Is that the part he plays in 'Above Stairs'? Well, you are obviously a fan."

"I am not! I have never watched it before. And I wasn't pointing the finger at Lawrence. Just, I mean, if he saw Gordon Wright after he left the Cat and Fiddle then, well, that is important. Yes?"

"Yes. It is. Very important."

"And?"

"And what? Jess, I hope you aren't playing detective again. Last time almost got you killed."

There was a pattern emerging. He only called me Reverend Ward when he was being all official and Jess when it was more personal. Did I detect a note of concern? Maybe he was not as angry as he seemed. Perhaps, my sister's charms hadn't worked this time. I mean any man would be flattered but he could see through her, right? He said he thought I had more substance. I could still retrieve this situation if I acted quickly.

"Inspector, Lawrence Pixley came over to see me last night after your visit. He was very anxious. He says that he didn't hurt Gordon Wright but got very distraught when he thought I had told you about their fight and then he ran off into the night. I think he knows more than he is letting on. I mean he was so worried that he walked from the school, along Back Lane and the graveyard without his coat."

"And? He was obviously in a hurry to speak to you. A man with a guilty conscience will make rash decisions."

"I don't know Lawrence that well, but he always has a handkerchief with him. One with his initials on it. A man with a hanky. A man with a seemingly constant battle with his sinuses doesn't forget to put his coat on in this weather. It is quite literally freezing out there."

"Very interesting. Well, thank you, Reverend, for coming in and bringing your family with you. I will let your memory lapse pass, this time. I won't keep you any longer."

Darn it, we are back to Reverend.

"No worries, Inspector, and I promise if I hear anything else you'll be the first to know."

"Thank you. And Jess, I was wondering." He nervously ran his finger inside his shirt collar. "Your sister, Zuzu, is she, erm, in a relationship?"

Double darn it!

Doctor, Doctor.

My Saturday morning rounds at the cottage hospital were a blessed relief after the tortured conversations over lunch and dinner following our family outing to the police station (or rather the incident room in the pub). The tension was not helped in any way by Zuzu announcing, as we packed away the evening's dishes, not to cook for her tomorrow because she had a date with 'Dishy Dave'.

"She called him 'Dishy'! Sam, I think I want to be sick."

"Hmmm, would you prefer Dreamy Dave or Drop-Dead Gorgeous Dave?"

"What about Don't Do it Dave! It's not fair! I saw him first!"

"Well, technically I did."

"*Did* you?"

"Well, maybe, a long time ago. We were at an emergency planning conference. It was an open bar. Look that doesn't matter. Are you going to talk to her? I am sure Zuzu would call it off if you asked her to."

I looked at my best friend with total incredulity. She was the one who first planted the idea that I might like 'Dishy Dave' knowing all along that she had a past with him. Now she was suggesting that all I had to do was tell my sister about my silly crush and everything would be okay.

"Why would I do that? He asked her, not me. He could've asked me. Several times he could have asked me."

"Then it's his loss. You'll find someone else. And you always have Jesus."

"Are you mocking me? I don't fancy my boss!"

"I didn't mean it like that, Jess. You have your faith. A certainty that the rest of us are desperate to find elsewhere. Here's me hunting for husband number three, and Zuzu? I saw her eyes undressing Leo. We need men. You don't. You are stronger than both of us."

"But I am not a nun, that's the other lot. I want someone to share my life with."

"Where would you put a man? That vicarage of yours is full as it is."

It was true. Despite the squabbles over the Smith inheritance, I was really enjoying spending time with my Mum and sister. I already missed Freya and was looking forward to her return at Easter. I was rediscovering my wider family, my old friends and making lots of new ones.

"Sam, you're right. I am extremely blessed. From now on my dealings with 'Dodgy Dave' will be purely professional. Like a bad dose of diarrhoea, I'll get over him."

"You are making him sound like a bad curry experience, but you go, sister!" Sam threw her hand in the air for a high five that I didn't catch and left her hanging. We laughed.

I gathered together my coat and stuff. There were still parishioners on my list to visit and I had better get a move on. I had a lot of walking ahead of me.

"Sam, I was just thinking. I don't suppose you know of anyone selling a scooter by any chance?"

Sal's Scooters

S am's advice had been to visit Salvatore Rossi's garage on the east end of the Wesberrey Road. There I was promised a cornucopia of Vespas, Lambrettas, Hondas and Piaggios. Scooters in all colours of the rainbow for all pockets. After my final round of the day, I jumped aboard the taxi carriage and headed down past Market Square and on through to the old industrial heart of Wesberrey, Stone Quay. Modern Stone Quay consists of artists workshops nestled alongside a couple of garages, a blacksmith, an appliance repair shop, farm equipment outlets, some builder's merchants and several boat chandlers. A tiny community of hands-on people and practical machinery. The quay itself is man-made, built in the early eighteenth century to provide a safe place to unload cargo to and from vessels heading from the mainland out into the English Channel and beyond. In the past, the area had a bit of a seedy reputation as merchant sailors made use of their ships' loading schedule to enjoy a little local entertainment. Once a thriving centre of commercial activity of all varieties, Stone Quay is now a relatively sleepy outpost. The introduction of steamboats and later diesel-powered ships removed the need for additional stops during a voyage and trade declined. What remains is a mossy stone wall jetty, a few weather-beaten buildings, and some rusty merchant yards.

The sky was overcast, and rain was definitely in the air, but as everyone knows the best way to cure a broken heart is to spend money. On the island, the most expensive thing I could throw my money at was an orange Lambretta V50 Special. 49cc of cool chic on two wheels with an automatic gearbox. All I had to do was sit on it and point myself in the right direction. Sal kindly threw in a matching helmet and the required 'L' plate for free and off I sped, keen to get home before sunset.

The journey home, with the first drops of rain spraying my face and the cold breeze whipping up around me as I cut through it, was exhilarating. I was now able to travel wherever I wanted, whenever I wanted. The headlamp in the front of Cilla (the name I decided to give my scooter) lit up the road ahead beautifully. Check me out, the runaway vicar. Born to be wild!

Zuzu's luggage was still somewhere en route from Rio, so she had been borrowing clothes from Freya, Mum and even on the odd occasion - me, despite her comments about my drab wardrobe. Today, she had slipped out on the early ferry to catch a train to Stourchester and its trendy boutiques. I walked in to find her doing an impromptu fashion show for my Mum, Cindy, and Hugo.

"Doesn't she look divine, darling." My aunt clapped her approval.

"Yes, yes, she does. As always. Is this for your hot date tonight?" I asked, doing my level best to un-grit my teeth.

"Yes, he is picking me up in an hour. I think these heels will make up it up to the Old School House. Of course, if one breaks on the way home, he'll just have to carry me!"

Zuzu danced around the kitchen like a teenager excited for her first Prom.

"The Old School House? You must tell us all about it when you return. I've always wondered how great the food must be there as they charge so much. Aunt Cindy, are you staying for dinner?"

"Of course, and I believe Pam is joining us too as Byron is at his model railway club, isn't that right, Bev?"

"Yes, I thought it would be nice to have a proper meal together before I go." Of course, my Mum would be leaving the island shortly. She only came for my collation. I had forgotten that she has a life pending elsewhere. I went over and hugged her around the shoulders and kissed her gently on the head.

"You don't have to go, Mum. You can stay as long as you like. Who's going to cook when you're gone?"

"Maybe you should advertise for a housekeeper, isn't that what vicars do?" Mum wriggled herself free from my embrace. She was never one for overt displays of affection and went to the fridge freezer. "I bought some lovely pork chops in town. As Zuzu isn't with us tonight, I thought we could ramp up the meat content."

"Sounds medieval! Jessie, you know you're my favourite sister. I was wondering, would you lend me those blue earrings you're always wearing? They'd go great with this dress, and I think they'll really bring out my eyes."

Normally one pitiful look from my sibling would have me handing over my worldly goods without question but not tonight.

"Zuzu, you know I would give you anything, but I promised Sam I would always wear them. What if you lost one? I would never be able to explain it to her. There were only two pairs made and therefore are irreplaceable."

"Sis, don't stress yourself. It's okay. Right, I'm off for a shower. See you later."

Well, that was easier than I thought. I should have added and 'please, don't take my man', but my name isn't Dolly Parton.

The doorbell rang on the dot of seven. With Mum busy in the kitchen pouring pink gins and my sister upstairs pouring herself into her new dress, it fell to me to answer the call.

"Inspector Lovington, my sister is nearly ready. Do you want to come in from the cold?"

"Please Jess, it's Dave. We're both off duty now. Lovely scooter, is that new?"

"Yeah. 'Cilla'. She's mine. Picked her up earlier."

Dave stepped over the threshold and stood nervously in the hallway, doing his best to make polite small talk while he waited. "Cilla, eh? Mmm, that smells delicious, perhaps we should stay here to eat?" His eyes sparkled at the thought of the pleasures of the night ahead. My eyes pricked with pain.

"Oh, but Zuzu has bought a new dress especially and trust me that dress needs to be taken somewhere special."

On cue, my sister appeared at the top of the stairs and slowly sashayed her way down. From the corner of my eye, I could see Dave wink. So that confirmed it, it was a nervous twitch, not part of any flirtation. I had to admit, though, that he had every right to be worried; my sister was dressed to kill.

"Dave Lovington! I had no idea you were my niece's date! Don't you both look handsome." Cindy emerged from the kitchen and shot me a surprised look. "Sorry, I was out when you called by earlier. I guess it was about the disappearance of Gordon Wright." He nodded. "Well, wherever he is it's very dark and very cold. I am afraid when you find him, he will be beyond help. Look, darling forget all about that now. If I see anything else, I will let you know. Have a wonderful evening."

Cindy made sure that the 'handsome' couple were well down the path before putting her arm around me and guiding me back towards the kitchen.

"Darling Jess, I didn't see that coming. I was sure he'd be more interested in you. Affairs of the heart are always difficult to read."

"Aunt, I told you I only see Inspector Lovington as a fellow professional. And you said it yourself, they make a very handsome pair." Cindy told me to sit down and placed a large gin glass in front of me. "What did you mean when you said Gordon Wright is somewhere cold and dark. Do you think he is dead?"

"Oh, my darling child, he has been dead for days!"

I looked across the oak table to see both my mother and Pamela nodding. Aunt Pamela reached out her hand to mine.

"Surely you can feel it? We had wondered, after the Well ceremony if you had..."

"Sorry, but no. How can I possibly feel if someone I barely know is alive or dead? Do you mean you all can? All three of you. Not just Cindy. Mum?"

"My gift is not as great as Cynthia's but yes, we can all tune in when we want to. I only have a sense of his energy, or rather the lack of his energy. Pam, you can feel more, can't you? There was a time we all thought Pam was the 'godmother' but then she got married and had a son."

"Yes," Cindy took up Pamela's outstretched hand. "Our mother, your grandmother, was convinced it was Pam. She had the gift, still has."

"It's a little rusty." Pam's face flushed.

"Yes, well Sis you need to practice. It's like any muscle." Cindy playfully patted her sister's hand. "Anyway, it wasn't until Mother died that my ability started to develop. I was a very late starter. A bit like you."

I slammed my glass down. "I am not a late starter. I am not psychic. I am not the next 'godmother'. This is all nonsense. Mum, aunts, I love you all very much, but can we let this drop. It's been a long day and I'm starving!"

And so began what turned out to be a very pleasant evening. It was lovely to see the three sisters relaxing together. Reminiscing over old times. Only very occasionally did my mind wander to my sister and her 'date'. About nine o'clock I thought it prudent to make my excuses and have an early night. I still had a sermon to finish for the next day and I didn't really want to be loitering when the 'handsome' couple returned. I heard them on the doorstep beneath my bedroom window about an hour later. I tried not to listen, but my sister has a brick piercing giggle. It sounded like they had a very good evening.

I was just about to turn off my bedside lamp and bury my head under the pillow when my mobile phone rang.

"Hello, Auntie Jess! Freya here. Just wanted to check you are all ok? I tried to call Mum, but it keeps going to voicemail."

"Yes, well she is a little busy at the moment. How are things back at uni?"

"Quiet. But that's somewhat of a relief, to be honest. I had a call from that police inspector. Is it true Gordon Wright has gone missing?"

"Yes, yes, it is. But I am sure he will turn up somewhere."

"Are you, really? Because I'm pretty sure he's in someone's freezer."

"Don't be silly Freya. You have a wild imagination."

"You're probably right. Don't know what I'm talking about. I just had this feeling when the inspector was on the phone. Can't shake it."

"Hmm, well I hope for his sake you are wrong. By the way, I bought myself a scooter. She's orange and I've called her Cilla."

"Ooh, lovely! That will help you whiz around the island. Saving souls on a moped! How's Hugo? I miss him."

"He misses you, too."

"Give him a cuddle, or maybe ask Mum to do it." She laughed. "I'd better go, Dom is trying to get me on WhatsApp."

Sunday Service

"Lawrence, I am so sorry about the other night. I think we got our wires crossed. You dropped this. Don't worry, it's been washed and freshly pressed."

I handed Lawrence a still warm handkerchief, the ironing of which was remembered just before I left for morning service. Lawrence Pixley was too preoccupied with arranging bleary-eyed school children into the choir stalls to engage in any conversation. He took the handkerchief, nodded, and stuffed it into his jacket pocket.

Thankfully, the service went well. The children were in fine voice and Rosemary's organ playing was restored to its usual flamboyance. I was surprised to see Arabella Stone in the congregation. Her gaunt features stared straight ahead throughout the mass. She was still in her seat when most of the parish had decanted to the village hall for refreshments. Only Tom and Ernest remained behind to collect the hymn books. I motioned to them to carry on ahead of me. Then I sat down next to Arabella and placed my hand on her shoulder.

"Arabella, are you okay? Do you want to have a cup of tea and a chat at the Vicarage?"

"Can I stay here a little longer?"

"Of course, do you want me to leave you to your thoughts?"

"No, Reverend. Can you stay?"

"Certainly."

We sat in silence.

"Your sermon today. It being St. Valentine's Day next week and all that. The power of loving relationships. Tell me, Reverend. What do you know about love?"

"I have been loved and I have loved."

"But have you ever been *in love*? Not just a fleeting fancy or a fondness but a gut-wrenching, insatiable need to be with someone else so much you can't imagine living without them? Doesn't make you a bad person, does it?"

She turned to look at me. Her eyes staring wildly, her pupils dilated.

"Arabella, have you taken something?"

"Who would blame me, eh? You? I wanted some love in my life. And I betrayed him. Now it's too late. Don't look at me like that. Who are you to judge?"

"I'm not judging you." I took both of her hands and held them firmly. "I only want to help."

"I thought he would help." Arabella tilted her head toward the figure of Christ on the cross above the altar. "But no one can. It's too late now."

"What do you mean too late?"

"He's dead."

"Who? Gordon?"

"No! PAPA!"

Arabella snatched her hands away. Throwing herself down on the kneelers in front she let out a soul-shattering wail.

***

Barbara and Phil rushed out from the hall to find me cradling a hysterical Arabella in the floor space between the two pews. Barbara leaned over and stroked Arabella's hair.

"Poor love, shall I fetch Dr Hawthorne?"

I nodded.

"You both stay 'ere. I'll run over to the Hospital." Phil protectively rubbed Barbara's back. "Looks like she needs a bit of TLC. One of your delicious cupcakes and a cup of sugary tea should do the trick."

"Right as always, Phil. I'll be straight back."

The excited chatter from the hall seeped into the dark church. My arms grew tired and the floor was cold, but Arabella clung tighter and tighter. Her tears finding a home on my green chasuble. Barbara returned with the promised refreshments and placed the tray down on the bench in front before helping me lift a still sobbing Arabella back up into her seat.

"Lord Somerstone has passed away," I whispered to Barbara, as she handed over a small plate of cakes.

"Oh my!" She knelt beside Arabella. "I remember when my father died. So much guilt. So much pain. Unlike anything else I have ever known."

Arabella took a sip of tea and winced. "How much sugar did you put in this?" She drank some more and bit into a vanilla cupcake. She became calmer. "Thank you."

"Do you want to talk about it?" Barbara squeezed her ample frame in beside Arabella at the edge of the pew, shunting us all up the bench a little.

"He died about one o'clock this morning. He didn't say anything. He was sleeping and then his breathing changed, and he went."

"I am sorry." Barbara and I looked over her bowed head and just smiled knowingly to each other. There are no suitable words at times like this, except you are sorry. What else can be said?

We sat together, all three sipping tea and eating cake until Phil returned with Sam close behind.

Bedside Manner

A sombre collection took an island taxi along Upper Road to Bridewell Manor. The gates were open when we arrived. Ralph, the butler and his wife Annie were standing on the steps leading up to the heavy front door. There was a deafening air of silence, even the birds appeared to be in mourning. The whole party made its way through the ornate hall and along a corridor which led into a fussy pink reception room that had obviously been converted into a makeshift hospital bed for Geoffrey Somerstone's last few months.

In the centre of the room, amidst dusty pink velvet sofas with buttoned backs and roll-top armrests and ornate gold painted tables with marble tops, stood stacks of National Geographic Magazines and The Times newspaper. In the centre of all this clutter sat a fully equipped hydraulic bed. On the bed lay the late Lord Somerstone. The room smelt strongly of bleach. In fact, the odour was quite overpowering.

Sam discreetly examined the body, confirmed he was dead and went off to the dining room to complete the death certificate. I could hear her call Leo Peasbody to arrange the body for collection. Ralph pulled up a chair for Arabella to sit on and then both he and Annie left us to prepare lunch. I said a few words and offered to stay if Arabella wanted some company.

"Reverend, someone needs to tell Tris." Arabella handed me her phone. "His House Master's number should be marked. The signal is better by the window."

I dutifully weaved my way around the stacks of paper and surplus furniture and left a message for Tristan to call his mother when he returned from a trip to the local village.

"I am sure he will be very upset to hear about his grandfather, especially with his own father missing as well. It will be very hard for both of you."

"Oh, I haven't told Tris about Gordon yet. No need to upset him when Gordon is likely to turn up at any moment. I'm sure the news of Papa's death will lure him out of whatever hole he's hiding in." Arabella was anxiously biting her nails.

"Arabella, when did you realise that Gordon was missing? I noticed he wasn't with you at Violet and Rachel's Funeral." I slowly edged my way back to the bed.

"We have separate rooms. I called his phone. No answer. So, I just left without him. He wasn't at dinner the night before, but as his *friends* had left that was no surprise. I just assumed he was dining elsewhere. After the funeral. After your mother told me what Hugh had said, I headed straight back here to confront him, and he was nowhere to be found. After trying his phone a few more times with no joy I called the police. To be honest, I had enough on my plate with Papa. Why don't you pull up one of those chairs? Just clear the magazines off. God, it will be a relief to chuck all this stuff away."

"And you have no idea where Gordon could be?" I took a pile of newspapers off a Louis XIV style chair (may even have been an *actual* Louis XIV chair for all I knew) and tried to lift it nearer to the bed. It appeared to be stuck to the parquet floor. With a bit of extra force, it jolted free. I positioned it at the side of the bed and walked around to sit down. The floor where the chair had stood felt a little tacky underfoot. I looked down and saw four small reddish-brown circles where the chair legs had stood. "Looks like something was spilt here at some point. Why are there so many back copies of the Times? The National Geographic I can understand but..."

"Papa loved to know what all his old chums were up to. His favourite page was the Obituaries. That reminds me, I need to make sure his entry is timely. He has it all written somewhere. Ralph will know where to find it."

"Ralph was very loyal to your father."

"Yes, he never left his side. He woke me up last night. Just in time. Oh dear, I shouldn't have brought Hugh here, against Papa's wishes. I betrayed his trust, even as he lay dying. I should have been here. Poor Ralph. he probably still hasn't slept. I just couldn't stay here, alone... it was too distressing. You understand, Reverend. Oh, I am such a terrible daughter! Ralph was an army medic, you see, before he became a butler. Such a blessing at the end. He did everything for Papa. I would have been lost without him, especially after Hugh left. Should I hold his hand? Papa's? It'll be cold, won't it?"

I nodded. "Only if you want to."

Arabella tentatively reached out her slim fingers to her father's. They touched briefly. "I can't. He's not there anymore, is he? Do you think he is watching?"

"There are many people who believe the spirit of a loved one hangs around for a few days, even months."

Arabella shivered.

There was a knock at the door. Sam came back in.

"Leo, sorry, Mr Peasbody said he will be over on the next ferry. I assume you will want your father to be placed in the family mausoleum?"

"Yes. A.S.A.P. Then seal the whole thing up. I want to be cremated. My ashes cast on the sea so I can continue to travel the world."

"Doctor, here you have my chair. I will go and check on what's happening in the kitchen."

Sam cast a look at me that suggested she would rather have a dose of water torture than sit with a corpse and make polite conversation with a grieving daughter. Her dealings with the dead and bereaved were usually quite short and matter of fact. But she still dutifully took my place at Lord Somerstone's side.

I wanted to take the opportunity to offer comfort to the late Lord's butler. I also thought I could find out more about Gordon Wright's disappearance from this loyal servant. I felt he would know more about the comings and goings at Bridewell than anyone.

Downstairs in the kitchen, I found that Ralph and Annie had been very busy. There were several plates of cold meats, cheese, and salad. Annie was stirring a pot of soup on the range cooker and Ralph was filling up a basket with warm bread rolls.

"I thought we could all eat here, Vicar. Save making up a table in the dining room. Do you think Lady Arabella would be happy with that arrangement?" Annie wiped her hands on her apron and reached across for a pair of oven mitts to lift the pot off the stove. "Ralph, sweetheart, can you put the trivet in the centre please."

Ralph placed a large circular cast iron stand on the centre of the table.

"I'll go and fetch Lady Arabella then. Please, Vicar, sit down and help yourself. We don't stand on ceremony below stairs."

Ralph looked like a man with the whole world on his shoulders. I doubt he had had any sleep for days.

"Annie, is there anything I can do to help? Drinks perhaps? Where do you keep the glasses? Shall we just have water? What about ice, do you have any in the freezer?"

"Ice?" Annie looked shocked at my suggestion. Maybe it was a little left-field given the temperature outside.

"Don't worry if it's too much trouble. Point me towards the freezer and I can get myself some."

Annie scuttled around to where I was standing and pulled out a chair.

"You will do no such thing, Vicar. You're a guest of her ladyship. Wait here. If you want ice. I'll go."

My eyes followed as Annie disappeared into the adjoining pantry. The soup smelled so good. Looking down the table I couldn't see any bowls, so I got up and starting to open some cupboards. I found the bowls in the far cupboard closest to the pantry. I couldn't see Annie. The freezer must be through in the next room. Or maybe they have an old-fashioned icehouse. I started to feel very guilty for putting her through so much trouble. Moments later Annie appeared at the doorway at the back of the room.

"There you go, Vicar. We keep the freezer out the back next to the walk-in chiller. It doesn't get used so much these days, not like when his Lordship entertained all the time. Do you think Lady Arabella will put some more life into this place? I am worried, Vicar, that she might spend all her time at her villa in Portugal. She used to hold such great parties."

"I think Arabella has many exciting plans for Bridewell," I reassured her and sat back down at the table, expectant bowl in hand. "The soup smells wonderful."

Not Jealous, Honest

"**J**ess, are you okay getting a taxi back to the vicarage? I need to escort Lord S back to the hospital with Leo." My gut response was not really but I also didn't want to be a cuckoo in the nest.

"Seriously, Sam. It's fine. There is still plenty of daylight left and I could do with a walk after all that soup."

"Not the three servings of apple pie and custard then?" My friend looked at me accusingly.

"Knowing what you are about to get up to with Mr Peasbody you are in absolutely no position to judge. Off you go then, and don't do anything I wouldn't do."

"Pah, that'll make for a very dull evening. Love you."

I watched the hearse drive away and started to wrap myself up for the walk ahead. Arabella was on the phone to her son and Annie was cleaning away the dishes, which left only Ralph to bid me farewell. Except he appeared to also be putting on his hat and coat.

"Hope you don't mind if I join you, Vicar. I could do with the air."

"Of course not. I would welcome the company."

We walked along in silence for a long time. I got the impression that Ralph had a lot of things on his mind. People often feel able to unburden themselves to me. The dog collar makes people relax. I felt he just needed a little nudge.

"Arabella was telling me how invaluable you have been during her father's illness. You will miss him a great deal I suspect."

"He was a great man, Vicar. I know he had a bit of a wild past. Who hasn't done things in their youth? But he was very good to me and Annie. He gave me a second chance. I would do anything for him. I did everything for him. Not sure what I am going to do now he has gone."

"I am sure Arabella will still want you and Annie to stay on and help run Bridewell. You mentioned a second chance. I need to start thinking about what I am going to say about him at his funeral. My family has mixed views about Lord Somerstone, it would be good to get a more rounded picture of the man and his legacy."

"It was Annie who introduced me to his Lordship. I had been discharged from the army. Stupid really. I loved military life, but people make mistakes. Mine was sneaking back onto barracks after curfew with a few joints in my back pocket. The RSM was just itching to get something on me. Next thing I knew I was NRFAS."

"Ralph, I'm sorry you have completely lost me RSM? NR?"

"NRFAS stands for Not Required For Further Army Service. RSM, Sergeant Major."

"Ah, so you were discharged for possession of drugs."

"Yes, things went from bad to awful and I ended up on the streets. I took refuge in the doorway of the club Annie worked at and she took pity on me. She, erm, used to help host some of his Lordship's parties and well, he needed a new butler and she gave him my name. He paid for me to go to school and study and I've been with him ever since. That was thirty years ago. Annie and I got married a few years later and she took up the role of cook and housekeeper when Lady Somerstone died."

"So, Bridewell is your home."

"And his Lordship, like a second father."

"So, you wouldn't want Bridewell to be turned into a hotel or anything like that?"

I had to ask. Seemed to me that Ralph would have clear cause to get rid of Gordon Wright if he heard about Gordon's business plans.

"Who would want to do that? Have you heard anything? Did Lady Arabella say that's what she planned to do? I suppose they might keep me on... but with my army record. Oh my! And my darling Annie. If they did any police checks."

Ralph grew extremely agitated. This was obviously a new idea to him, and his mind whizzed through all the possible scenarios. If he knew anything about Gordon's disappearance it wasn't related to the hotel. I reassured him that I was only speculating, and that Arabella hadn't mentioned anything about a hotel or any other plans.

When we got to the Vicarage Ralph leaned in and asked if he could give me a friendly hug. A rather strange request but he had just unburdened himself which often leads to a sense of bonding, so I agreed. I put my arms around his waist, and he embraced my back and shoulders. My head was facing out to the side, but I suddenly felt very short of breath like someone was holding a vacuum to my face. There was a white light and then I was back in the pink room, facing Geoffrey's bed. Except I wasn't there. I was looking in. Everything was muffled. I could see Lord S and the shadow of another man. He was standing over the bed and then he jumped back. Everything went dark.

"Vicar, Vicar? Are you okay?"

Ralph was holding me up. I must have fainted.

"Yes, Ralph. I'm fine. I just, I don't really know. Please, can you help me inside."

A Night of Discovery

"Don't fuss. I'm okay. I was just a little faint, that's all. Please, just a sip of water and a bit of peace and quiet is all I need."

Mum steered me into the morning room and sat me down on the sofa.

"Jess, did you see anything? When you fainted. Do you remember what you saw?"

"Mum, how did you know? Oh, it doesn't matter." I looked around to see if anyone had followed us into the room. "It was really quite scary. Like a bad dream. There was a man. Well, I think it was a man. More of a shadow. Leaning over Geoffrey Somerstone. Then the figure... well, it kind of bent back on itself, like it had been cut in two."

"You do understand what you saw, don't you?" Mum had pulled over a footstool and was perched on the edge leaning forward, her hands knitted together. "This is how it starts. Coming back here. Visiting the well. You are starting to reconnect."

"Mum, it was probably a sugar crash after the long walk home. I had too many apple pies. Then the bear hug."

"And it scared you because it felt so real. I understand. I will be in the kitchen if you need me. I will leave you alone for a while. That poor man got such a fright!" She stood up and kissed me gently on the forehead.

I pulled the footstool across and lifted my feet up to rest on it. If it was a vision, of course that was crazy but, if it was a vision then what exactly did I see? Was the shadow the dutiful Ralph? Maybe he couldn't accept seeing his master suffering so decided to hasten his end. Or was it Arabella? What was the shadowy figure doing? Was it a final kiss goodbye? And why did the figure collapse in on itself? Anguish maybe or guilt. I felt pain. I felt 'it' was in pain.

I snuggled my body down into the shape of the chair and closed my eyes. It was time for a quiet moment of prayer. Prayer became meditation and meditation became a deep sleep. When I emerged back into the real world the night had closed in. The moon was casting his reflective glow through the French windows and the whole room had adopted a slightly blue tint. I stretched my way off the sofa and followed the homemade cooking trails leading me up the hall. The bright artificial lights of the kitchen seared through my half-closed eyelids, and I couldn't see a thing. Just voices and shapes that morphed slowly into people. One of the shapes took a while to reconstitute itself. It was male. Casually dressed. A bright red shirt. Was that a pencil moustache? Oh no, Zuzu had a second date!

I staggered to the fridge and pulled out a jug of orange juice. Zuzu stepped in to block my escape.

"Check out his top! The equestrian print. I am sure it's Gucci." my sister whispered admiringly. "Retails around £800. That man has class!"

"Or a trust fund! Seriously who pays that much for one shirt. Looks a bit flashy to me." I snapped back, casting an eye over to check just how ghastly it was. "So, two nights back-to-back. You must have had a great first date."

Zuzu lifted her glass of wine to cover her mouth as she spoke. Fortunately, Dave was busy making friends with Hugo. "Jessie, I had the best time ever. He is so giving. I could have anything I wanted from the menu. A lady came in selling roses. He bought her whole stock! You should see my bedroom, it's like the dressing room of a prima ballerina on opening night. I smell old money. Not brash with it. He was just the perfect gentleman. Great sense of humour. He kissed me on the hand. The hand! I am hoping to get to first base tonight, at least." She giggled and snorted at the same time. "Ooh, must be the bubbles in this Prosecco. I'm feeling incredibly giddy."

Zuzu brushed my arm gently. Then she slinked across the kitchen to claim her man, casually picking up an olive from the counter to suggestively pop into her mouth as she went. It had occurred to me when I first met the Inspector that he had slightly more than his police detective's salary to play with. His Burberry trench coat looked original, and his suits always fitted him perfectly. Fashion is not my thing. Zuzu, however, had made a study of money and its matching accessories all her life. Maybe they were a perfect match.

My mother certainly seemed to approve. She had convinced them to dine with us instead of another evening of overpriced steaks at the Old School House. I was very tempted to use my fainting spell as an excuse to have an early night, but the die was cast. Dishy Dave was off the menu for me but why should I let that make me miss out on one of my mother's famous fish pies.

"More wine, Vicar!" My sister laughed. "That sounds like a line from one of those amateur farces. You know the ones where they keep missing each other in the gazebo."

"Talking about missing people, do you have any more leads on Gordon Wright, Inspector?"

"Mrs Ward, please. I'm off duty but I'm afraid it's not looking good. There doesn't appear to have been any sightings of Mr Wright after he left Lawrence Pixley. His bank cards haven't been used and there is no signal from his mobile phone. I think your sister is right in her suggestion that when and if we find Mr Wright it will be too late."

"Cynthia is always right, Inspector. I understand you used her talents before when your wife died."

His wife! He had a wife. He has a dead wife! And my mother and Cindy knew about it! Is there anything else I don't know about? Tom and Ernest are Russian spies perhaps or Uncle Byron is actually working on nuclear fusion in his shed at the back of the garden, not a model railway. I knew there was something. When I first saw Dave speaking to Cindy, they were very secretive. Did she help him talk to his wife from the grave? If so, what happened to her? So many questions to ask but Zuzu got in first.

"I didn't realise you were married. A widower. That's so sad."

Dave sunk in on himself. His puppy eyes grew misty.

"April died ten years ago. Feels like yesterday. And before you ask, yes, we had children. Twins. A girl and a boy. Lucy and Rupert. Both on their gap year. They live with their grandmother. My job doesn't allow for successful parenting, not on your own. And I still miss her. Everyday."

A quick glance at my sister told me that every word Dave said just endeared him to her more. He was handsome, professional, rich and, even better, a lonely widower with long-distance children. I could sense her mentally wrapping herself around him. Offering him her own special brand of comfort.

The meal over, Mum and I made our excuses and left Zuzu and Dave to finish the remaining bottle of wine. When we got to the top of the stairs Mum gave me a gentle squeeze on my right hand. I wasn't quite ready to say goodnight. Something was still bugging me.

"Mum, you said Cindy helped Dave when his wife died. How did she die?"

"Oh dear, it was very tragic. Cindy was telling me yesterday. Poor man. It was suicide. Just off the coast here. She just walked out to sea and drowned.

Teachers Need Love Too

As expected of a true gentleman, I heard Dave leaving to get the last taxi carriage to Market Square just before eleven-thirty. His departure was quickly followed by my sister stumbling up the hall stairs to her room and muttering to Hugo.

"You'll come to bed with me, won't you? You handsome devil, you. Ssshh, we'll wake everyone up. Things are defin-definat-totally looking up, my furry friend. I think this one's a keeper. And not a stinking fluffy-headed whatsit in sight — except for you of course."

My sister was less vocal over breakfast.

"I see someone had a bit too much to drink last night. There, there. Sit yourself down. I'll make you some coffee poppet. Jessamy, another one for you?"

"No thanks, Mum. I need to prepare for the school assembly. Which won't be at all awkward with Lawrence Pixley thinking I ratted him out to the police!"

"You sure do have a strange way of making friends, Jessie." My sister reached over to grab a stick of crispy bacon.

"Oi! I thought you were a pescatarian!" I said, slapping the bacon out of her hand with my knife.

"Today, I am a flexitarian. That bacon smells too good. Mum! Could you cook me some, please?"

"What are you two going to do when I go back home, eh?" My mother playfully ruffled Zuzu's bed hair and went to get some more bacon out of the fridge.

I leant across and softly asked my sister if the night had been as successful as she wished.

"Do you mean, did we get to first base? Totally. And we had a bit of a rummage around second as well." Zuzu took advantage of my shock to grab another slice of bacon. "Look at your face! Don't be such a prude, Jessie. I promise no further. Not in your house. That would be unseemly." She laughed.

I was happy for her. Really, I was.

My reception at Cliffview Primary School was even chillier than last time. Audrey Matthews was sporting dark maroon-purple nail polish, though I had very little opportunity to admire her manicure as the black register was snatched away even quicker than before.

"How you could think Mr Pixley was in any way associated with the disappearance of Gordon Wright is, well, quite incomprehensible."

"But Audrey, you told Stan, who told me, and it was important that the police learnt, that Gordon was here. I didn't suggest that Lawrence had anything to do with it. I never meant to get him in trouble. He seemed okay at mass yesterday."

"And how would you know eh? Based on a half-hour meeting discussing melodicas you think you know him. You think you could possibly understand a man as sensitive and intelligent as Mr Pixley. I called your number right from the get-go. Lady vicar, coming here from the mainland. Thinks she's better than us. Sticking her beak into everybody's business. I warned Stan and I've warned Mr Pixley. "

"Audrey, I think we just got off on the wrong foot. I would like us to start again. Maybe even be friends."

"No thank you, Reverend Ward. I have plenty of friends who I can trust not to go scuttling off to the coppers with everyone's secrets. We are a close community here, Vicar. Best watch your step."

"Audrey, please, I —"

"Mrs Matthews to you, please, Reverend Ward. If you don't mind, I have lots of work to do. Sit over there and Mr Pixley will take you through to the hall when they are ready.

Fortunately, I wasn't waiting long. Soon I was the focus of attention for just over a hundred and fifty young children. The theme of the assembly was St Valentine.

"Morning everyone. Now, who can tell me about St Valentine's Day?"

One hand, attached to a cherubic boy on the front row, shot up.

"Hi, and what's your name?"

"Oscar, Miss."

"Oscar, lovely. So can you tell me about St. Valentine's Day?"

"Yes, Miss it's the day my dad buys my mum lots of chocolates that she can't eat 'cos she's on a diet. So, I get them all. But he doesn't know, Miss. It's our secret. Last year he bought some really funny tasting ones with liquid centres. Lickers or something. I was sick for a week!"

"Oh my! Thank you, Oscar. Anyone else?"

"Yes, Miss. Me, Miss!"

"And your name is?"

"Charlie, Miss."

"Charlie. So, what does St. Valentine's mean for you?"

"It means all the soppy girls are going to be crying 'cos they never got a card! They're just stupid, Miss."

"You're stupid!" several of the girls called out in response.

"Thank you, Charlie. No one is stupid. But people do get upset when they expect something nice and then it doesn't happen. But chocolates and cards are not the reason for celebrating St. Valentine's Day. It's not about gifts. It's about love. The Bible says that God loves us. In fact, it says that God loves us so much that he sent Jesus to show us what God is like and to show us God's love. Now, how do you think we can show our love for God?"

Silence. There was some shuffling of bottoms from sitting crossed legged for too long on the wooden floor, but no hands in the air. Onwards.

"By being careful about what we say, by saying nice things to other people, and by being helpful and doing kind things. So, this Valentine's Day I want you to do something nice for someone that you love. Maybe your Mum, Dad, a grandparent, a friend. Maybe even a teacher."

The last suggestion received a few boos from the back row.

"Yes, your teachers need love too. Everyone needs love and it's free to give."

I nodded to Lawrence to let him know I was finished. He encouraged everyone to give me a round of applause. Then we sang 'Give me joy in my heart'. There are always some children who really belt out the *sing* in the 'Sing Hosanna' chorus.

I hung back whilst the rows of children shuffled back to their lessons, the smallest ones first.

"Jess, you will pop back to the office with me for a cup of tea, or coffee if you prefer, before you go."

"I am not sure Mrs Matthews would be very happy with me taking up any more of your valuable time."

"Oh, don't mind Audrey. She just looks out for me. I want to explain to you a bit more about what happened with Gordon Wright. Of course, if you have to be somewhere else, we could..."

It surprised me that Lawrence wanted to pick up on our aborted conversation from the other night. I sensed that he had more he wanted to confide in me. I felt both honoured and curious. "I would be delighted to join you for tea, Lawrence. Lead on."

Initially, it seems Gordon was boasting about how he would soon be in a position to be a major benefactor to the school. He joked that perhaps they could change the name from Cliffview Primary to the Gordon Wright Academy. However, Lawrence went on to explain that Gordon turned very defensive when the conversation diverted onto the subject of cheap materials being used in the school's construction.

"Jess, he told me not to speak of such things ever again and how dare I besmirch his father's good name. He told me that I didn't understand business and finance. I reminded him that as a headteacher I am always seeking to get value for money. My budgetary skills are a match for any corporate chief executive. That it didn't take a genius to work through a set of accounts. It was then that Gordon Wright's mood changed. He shouted at me. Told me I didn't understand. He used language that should never be heard in a school. When I tried to stand my ground, he shoved me. I'm ashamed to say I shoved him back. I believe that is what Audrey saw. I pushed him quite hard, and he lost his balance a little but that was all. He wasn't hurt."

"Then he left?"

"Yes. I felt awful and I was so worried. I mean the school needs his investment. I had to go after him."

I was suddenly very anxious about what Lawrence was going to admit to next.

"So, you followed him?"

"Yes, but not immediately. I waited for everyone to leave and locked up as usual. Then I rode up to the manor house on my bicycle."

"How much time had elapsed would you say?"

"Oh, no more than ten or fifteen minutes. It's a good thirty-minute walk to Bridewell from here so I knew I would catch up with him."

I scanned Lawrence's face for any trace of anxiety or fear but found none. In fact, he was uncharacteristically calm. I noticed he had stopped sniffing.

"So, did you?"

"Did I what?"

"Catch him."

"Yes, well no actually. Almost."

The frustration I was beginning to feel with this conversation was palpable.

"Lawrence, you can trust me. Please just cut to the chase. What happened?"

"Nothing. I promise you, Jess. Absolutely nothing happened. I rode as fast as I could and made good time, but I missed him. I mean when I got there the big security gates were locked. There was no one on the gate, fortunately, because after the ride I, well, I didn't feel the need to continue our conversation. I could see him walking up the path to the main door. It was dark but it was clearly him. Anyway, I just turned the bike around and headed back down Upper Road."

"You mean to tell me that Gordon Wright went back to Bridewell Manor!"

"Of course, where else would he go?"

I had to tell the Inspector. Did the security guard in the gatehouse let Gordon in? If so, he could corroborate Lawrence's story. But if he did, why hasn't he come forward with that information already? Though Lawrence said there was no one on the gate, was there another way in? Either way, my hunch was that someone at Bridewell Manor was lying. Someone there knew what had happened to Gordon and where he was.

Dancing Nymphs

It had started to rain. A light, soft rain gently kissed the grey headstones and the graveyard's furry inhabitants as I weaved my way back to the vicarage. Some of the drier cats had found shelter under the overhang of the Somerstone's mausoleum, others in the hollow trunks of nearby trees. The poor mites must be so cold and yet they seemed reasonably happy snuggled tight together in whatever warm corner they could find.

Though it was not even midday, the sky was dark, and the lights of the vicarage were already on. Zuzu greeted me at the door.

"Seems you are Miss Popular today. There is quite a gathering. I put them all in the morning room, as that is the most decent space. Well, except for those ghastly fish eyeballing everyone from the sideboard."

"So, who's here?"

"Dave, but in an official capacity. Arabella, Barbara, Sam, and that handsome undertaker."

"Leo Peasbody? Okay, I assume this is about the arrangements for Geoffrey's funeral. Is Mum around?"

"Yes, she is in full hostess mode." Zuzu straightened up and bowed. With a snigger, she added, "Luncheon will be served at noon."

"Oh, stop it! Though you would make a great butler, maybe I will have an opening."

I took off my coat and a layer of winter accessories and took a few seconds to check out exactly how red my nose was in the hall mirror before entering the fray. I bumped into Barbara who was partially blocking the door to the morning room.

"Don't mind me, Vicar. I'll go and help your mother with the sandwiches. Lady Arabella would like to discuss having her father's funeral on Friday. I have already checked your diary. We can manage that. It's short notice but I will speak to the florist and Rosemary about the organ. Get the ball rolling. I'll leave you to talk through the finer details." I nodded permission to leave, allowing Barbara to bid a hasty retreat to the warmth of the kitchen. She touched my shoulder on the way out. I think she was grateful to escape.

"So, Valentine's Day. That is quick. Inspector, will Lord Somerstone's body be available that soon?"

"Dr Hawthorne here has confirmed he died of natural causes. With Lady Somer-stone-Wright's husband still missing, I see no need to cause any unnecessary suffering with further delay. I did want to speak to you, Reverend, on a different matter but I can wait outside. I will see you in, say half an hour." With that he left, bowing respectfully to Arabella on his way out.

And then there were three.

"I just popped by to see how you were." Sam was sat next to Leo on the sofa, her long legs wrapping themselves in his direction, she pulled down her pencil skirt inevitably drawing more attention to her slender thighs. A quick glance at Leo confirmed that he had noticed too. "Mr Peasbody and Arabella were here when I arrived. The Inspector came in shortly afterwards. All the necessary paperwork is done." Sam started to nervously fiddle with her left earring. "I can join the others in the kitchen if you wish?" I had the feeling Sam was very keen to stay as close to Leo as possible.

"I am more than happy for you to stay, my friend. If that is ok with Arabella?"

"Of course, perhaps, Dr Hawthorne you can help me pick out hymns for the service. I am not much of a churchgoer. Mr Peasbody, my father will expect the best but nothing sentimental. He loved beautiful things. Your secretary, Barbara? She suggested calla lilies. I think that would look beautiful, with white orchids perhaps. Just white, everything white." Arabella was very composed, if sombre. Not surprising given recent events. As always, she was extremely elegant in her black dress and short jacket with cord trim. In fact, everyone looked immaculate, I was the only one in the room looking a little weather worn.

"I will unseal the mausoleum on Thursday evening. As we opened it for Violet and Rachel Smith just a week ago, there is very little to do in preparation. Lord Somerstone's tomb was already identified. We can have a nameplate made on the mainland within twenty-four hours." Despite the temptation sitting next to him, Leo remained professional. "While we were waiting for you, Reverend, I discussed the casket with Lady Arabella. I think I have all the information I need. There is one unusual request that I said we would need to get your permission for." At this point, Leo's slick persona became a little less comfortable.

"I am intrigued, pray do continue. I am sure we can meet any request."

Leo looked anxiously to Arabella. She girded herself. "My father made very few last requests. There was no mention of hymns, flowers, poems or what have you. But he did make one. There was a dancing club he liked to visit in Stourchester, 'Aphrodite'. I believe our housekeeper, Annie used to work there many years ago. Well, it seems they have a signature routine they perform every night. All the dancers in the show take part. Well, my father's last request was that they perform this dance at his funeral."

"This 'club'," I gasped, "do the dancers wear, I mean, are they, erm, exotic dancers?"

"Technically, yes. But they will remain clothed. This dance, it seems is very tasteful. They performed for my father's last birthday up at Bridewell. I was in Portugal, but I spoke with Annie, she assures me it is very respectful. They are dressed as Greek muses, representing the arts and so on. Nine of them carrying harps and lyres and stuff. The muses are carved on the outside of the family tomb. It's something of a family tradition."

"I thought they were nymphs!"

Sam was quick to jump onto my ignorance.

"They are much the same; nymphs are more associated with a location like woodland, mountains etcetera, whereas muses have a role."

"But still pagan." I shuddered. I believe in a modern church that embraces all cultures, and I knew there were already pagan references in the history and fabric of the abbey, but dancing nymphs was possibly a step too far. "It's such short notice, maybe the ladies have other plans for Valentine's Day?"

"Oh, I have already been in touch. They said they would be delighted. They all knew my father very well."

I am sure they did. Maybe I really am a prude like Zuzu thinks, but this is the house of God! I looked at Arabella, who I had grown to have a good deal of affection for over the past few weeks. We have very different views of the world, but this was my father's best friend's last request, was it really my place to judge his wishes and deny him such a trivial thing?

"Okay, you have my permission, but they must be respectfully attired."

Arabella jumped up and hugged me. I hugged back.

It didn't take long to confirm the other arrangements for the service and soon we were in the kitchen standing with plates in hand, munching on ham salad sandwiches and a range of freshly chopped crudités and dips.

I slowly manoeuvred my way towards the Inspector who, as you would expect, was in deep conversation with my sister.

"Inspector, you wanted to speak to me?"

"Yes, Reverend. Shall we go to your study?"

We made our excuses to the impromptu lunch guests and walked in silence down the hall. I marvelled to myself how soon I had accepted the official nature of our relationship. Only a few days earlier I would have been coyly planning something clever to say in a ridiculous attempt to impress my crush. Now I see that that was all it was.

I sat myself down at my desk and invited Dave to take a seat.

"So, Inspector, how may I be of assistance?"

"Reverend, I had wanted to test out your feelings about Gordon Wright's marriage. It seems to be a rather strange setup."

"Well, you know the British aristocracy, normal rules of life don't seem to apply to them."

"We're not all like that."

Oh my heavens! Inspector Dave Lovington of the Stourchester constabulary is one of 'them', the British aristocracy. He is a blue-blooded member of the thin blue line.

"Sorry, Inspector. I had no idea. No offence meant."

"None taken. I am the fourth son of a baronet. It's hardly worth a mention. I have no title, no land - just a lot of issues. Now, Arabella and Gordon. Not a match made in heaven, I understand."

"No, it was a marriage of convenience. Gordon brought the money and Arabella the title and the big estate."

"Except, there is no money. Well very little. It seems Hugh Burton was right about Mr Wright's associates. Let's just say they are the first generation of *respectable* businessmen in their families. Their fathers knew the Kray twins very well."

"So, they are gangsters. But it makes no sense to get rid of Gordon before Lord Somerstone's death."

"And I am almost certain they didn't. My team looked very carefully into their movements after they took the ferry. They both have perfect alibis and when interviewed appeared to be seriously worried about their 'friend'."

"Or worried about losing their business venture." I thought this would be a good opportunity to share what Lawrence had told me about Gordon returning to Bridewell after their little scuffle. "I would have mentioned it immediately but, well everyone was here, and you made a quick exit to the kitchen so..."

"Jess, erm Reverend." He coughed. "Please don't apologise. I suppose we will need to get accustomed to mixing business with pleasure if I continue to see your sister."

My heart only wept a little bit.

"I am sure we will work things out. Let's make the study the business zone and the kitchen the pleasure zone. Do you think you will be seeing a lot more of my sister then?"

"Oh, I really hope so, Jess. After my wife passed away, I never thought I would ever want to be with anyone else, ever. But Zuzu... I know it's early days, but may I confide in you. As a friend?"

Oh dear, was I ready to hear this? I nodded.

"I think I might be falling in love."

Forty Winks

Fortunately, the next forty-eight hours went by with minimal drama, no strange voices or visions and no further declarations of undying love. Parish life moved along much as one would expect with the normal round of visits to sick and elderly parishioners, made a lot easier with the help of Cilla.

I knew from talking through the final funeral arrangements with Arabella over the phone that the police had been to Bridewell to interview the security guard and other staff about their last sightings of Gordon. Lawrence had popped in on his way back on Tuesday to tell me about giving a full statement to PC Taylor in the incident room in the Cat and Fiddle.

He seemed relieved to have got that weight off his chest. And Zuzu had provided me with daily updates of her conversations with Inspector Lovington, though it seems they rarely talked about his work. The only person I hadn't seen or heard much of was Sam. I imagined that she was busy with work and making time for Leo Peasbody. Was it selfish to hope for no more funerals for a while only because I missed the evening chats with my friend?

Mum had announced over breakfast that she would be heading home on Saturday morning. I was going to miss her so much. I had left home over thirty years ago to try and make my name as an actress. The car crash and my severe lack of talent, soon put pay to that but once I had left home there was no going back.

My mother and I had a strong relationship. She was always there when I needed her, but this was the longest we had lived together under one roof for over three decades and I liked it. I enjoyed just doing normal, routine things together like cooking breakfast, washing the dishes, or taking food up to the graveyard for our feral friends. Simple, little things.

I had lived on my own for such a long time. Even when I shared a priest's house, it's much like a student flat. You are together but you know it is temporary. You are friends but not family. Colleagues, not blood. Strangers, not relatives. With family, you can truly relax. I was happy.

That is not to say it was a bed of roses. Mum and Zuzu clashed every day over the rights and wrongs of accepting money from either Violet Smith or Lord Somerstone's estates. Now that Lord S was dead, the trust fund he had set up in our name would pay up if we could convince my younger sister to return to Wesberrey.

Around three o'clock, whilst I was contemplating a sneaky forty winks on the chaise lounge in my study, the phone rang in the hall. Slowly, and I will admit slightly reluctantly, I dragged myself up and creaked towards the door. Very few people called the landline anymore and I was quite tempted to let it go to answerphone. In contrast, Zuzu dashed to the phone like a greyhound out of the stocks, picking it up within three rings.

"Rosie? Where are you? Speak up! Is that a train whistle? Are you in a station? Of course, what do you need? Give me your account details and I will ping you the money. Mum! Mummy! I need a pen and some paper."

I opened the door to see my mother handing Zuzu a notepad. Her face etched with concern. "It's Rosie." She mouthed to me. I walked over and pulled her in towards me.

"Ok. I have all your details. I will send this across straight away. What time should we expect you? I will come to the ferry. Is Luke with you? Okay. Everything will be fine. We are all here."

Zuzu put the phone down and turned to us with a sly smile. "Teddy has run off with his secretary. Seems he has cleaned out their joint bank account. The business trip to New York was just a ruse. The first thing Rosie knew was when the bailiffs turned up at the factory. She hasn't a bean to her name!"

"There's no need to look quite so happy!" snapped my mother. "My baby girl! Where is she now?"

"At Kings Cross, she needs the train fare. Looks like you are going to have some new house guests, Jessie." Zuzu tapped my shoulder as she strode past to get her phone from the kitchen. Mum and I followed behind.

"Mum, let me make you a nice cup of tea whilst Zuzu sorts out the money transfer. Don't worry, Rosie will be here soon. She can have Freya's room and Luke can have the spare, though I haven't changed the sheets since Cindy stayed over. It was just one night. We have time to work it out."

"Bloody men! Bastards, the lot of them. My poor Rosebud. She worked so hard to build that business up." My mother grabbed a clean tea towel from the nearby dresser drawer to wipe away her tears.

"Mum, let me get you a tissue, or some toilet roll even."

"Don't be silly, what a waste of trees. This is clean, it will do. Why did she call the landline?"

"Rosie said she lost her phone. All she had on her was the leaflet you sent her from Jessie's Welcome Service. That had the vicarage number on it. She was calling from a booth."

"But she has her purse, her bank cards?"

"Yes, she has one of her own, but it didn't have enough on it for the train. All the joint cards have been frozen."

"Oh, my poor baby!"

So, Rosie was coming home, just as Cindy predicted.

MAUSOLEUM MADNESS

Bloody Men!

It was close to midnight before my devastated sister and her son were safely gathered at the kitchen table that was now offering them a secure respite from the horror of the last few days. Slowly Rosie relayed how she had learnt about her husband's infidelity and the bankruptcy. It was a lot to take in. It was shocking to see my baby sister a crumpled version of her usual competent self. Everyone else knew it was her that was the backbone of their business and their marriage. None of us ever really understood what she had seen in Teddy. He had an ability to command her and manipulate her that went beyond his obvious outward charms and good looks. He was a chancer and a brute and Rosie had spent her adult life sorting out his mistakes. Now, she sat across from me at the Vicarage table. A ghost of the vibrant young woman I had been chief bridesmaid for, in that hideous peach dress, all those years ago.

Luke, always a sickly-looking boy anyway, appeared to be disappearing into his grey hoodie. His large dark eyes were the only indicator that he was there at all.

"Can I go to my room now?" he growled.

"Yes, of course. It's a bit on the small side, not much more than a box room." I could see the stoicism on his young face. Luke had lost a lot. His friends. His home. "Just for now, eh? We can clear some space in the attic later and you can have your own private den. The mattress up there was full of mildew. I doubt that room has been aired in decades." He

120

sniffed as he nodded, there was possibly even a tear. "We'll sort you out a proper bed up there in due course. I promise. Here, let me take your stuff, follow me." I picked up Luke's rucksack and lead him to his bed for the night. "I'm sorry it's not much. Can I get you a glass of water?" Luke shook his head.

"Do you have an Xbox? Or a PlayStation?" His look told me he had already resigned himself to the answer being no. "Never mind, I have my iPad. You do have the internet?"

"Yes, I will get you the code."

"K."

"K?"

"Yes. O.K!"

Luke pulled back his hood and shook out a mass of black curls. I hoped that his hair and spectral features were all he had inherited from his father. I remembered how Rosie used to draw pictures of Teddy when they first met. There was no denying he had a hauntingly beautiful face, one that my sister studied in great detail. I had always wished though that he had a beautiful personality to match. Teddy was a serial philanderer and a bully who exploited my sister's devotion and loyalty, but she adored him. In fact, I doubt she would have ever decided to leave him. Now it seems he had made the decision for her.

"Ah, right. K. I will be back in a minute. Just make yourself at home."

After taking the code up to my nephew I went back to the kitchen. Zuzu was texting someone on her phone. From the way she was biting her lip, I guessed it was Dave. Mum and Rosie were both sat at the other end of the kitchen table, cradling cups of tomato soup in their hands. No one was speaking.

"Rosie, why don't I take you up too. You need to sleep. We can decide what to do next in the morning."

She nodded and silently gathered her suitcase and a large handbag. That was all she had with her. All she had to show for twenty years of marriage.

I had made up a fresh bed for Rosie in the room that Freya had stayed in at the far end of the landing. The room featured a small double bed encased in a mahogany bed frame which beautifully matched the regency writing desk and chair by the box window and the small wardrobe in the recess by the chimney breast. On the other side stood an odd little mid-century teak chest of drawers and, at the end of the bed, an ottoman chest covered in a green damask fabric. It was a room filled with authentic charm, but I don't think my sister was in the right mood to appreciate it.

"Do you have anything that needs hanging up? All the drawers and so on are empty. Just make yourself at home. I've put some towels for you on this chair. Do you need anything else?"

"Yes, hold on." Rosie unzipped her handbag and rummaged around inside, pulling out a cream envelope. "Can you throw this in the bin. Better still, can you burn it? Thanks, Sis."

"No worries, what is it?"

"A Valentine's card. For Teddy."

Rosie slumped down on the bed and threw herself face down onto the pillows. They weren't enough to muffle her tears. I sat down beside her and stroked her hair, just like I did forty years ago when our father died.

Mum was right. Bloody men!

Muses and Mayhem

It had been a late and stressful night for all of us. A peaceful, leisurely morning was much needed but was not to be. The house was awoken by thunderous knocking on the front door around eight a.m. An overzealous delivery boy had in his cart a dozen bunches of red roses. I doubt he had ever had to deliver so many blooms to one woman. That lucky lady, of course, was my sister Zuzu whose squeals of delight woke anyone who had managed to sleep through the knocking.

"A dozen bunches! I don't think we have enough vases. There will be some in the hall but we need them for Lord S's funeral. I get it's a grand gesture of love but not very practical."

"You're just jealous!"

Zuzu was probably right. Ever resourceful, my mother suggested that we run some water in the bath and put them in there temporarily.

"Right, let's get the kettle on. We have a busy day ahead of us all. Jessamy, you have an important funeral. Zuzu, you must find proper homes for all those flowers and Rosie, we need to get you to a solicitor."

Slightly late to the party, Luke flopped down the stairs, rubbing his eyes.

"And what am I meant to do here? The internet sucks."

"Luke, why don't you come and help me prepare for the funeral? I know it's not much fun but tomorrow we can catch the ferry and go get that gaming thing you wanted. An Xbox, right? The funeral promises to be a grand affair we even have dancing girls."

"At a funeral?" Rosie was trying to untangle some of her son's wayward locks, though he kept squirming away. "What kind of dancing girls? Like a school troop? Majorettes or something?"

"Oh, I wish! No, these ladies are exotic dancers from the Aphrodite club in Stourchester. They are going to be muses."

From under his curly fringe, I could see a flicker of interest enter Luke's teenage eyes.

"Do I have to wear black, as it's a funeral? Not a problem, nearly everything I own is black. But I don't have a suit. If you need me to wear a suit, then..."

"Just be smart. Black is perfect. Mum, are you attending?"

"Wild horses wouldn't keep me away. Muses! He never changed, did he? That man had the libido of a rabbit! Now, who wants scrambled eggs?"

The rest of the morning's preparations went smoothly. I suggested to Rosie that she had a quick chat with Ernest to get some informal legal advice in the short term and that she would find him at one end or the other of the cliff railway. Zuzu volunteered to escort our sister. I think she was also keen to alert Ernest to the fact that Rosie had returned. Luke turned out to be a pretty useful gofer. I sensed that he enjoyed having things to do. Once Barbara and Phil realised he was keen to try his hand at anything, they managed to devise quite a list of odd jobs between them. The funeral was set for one o'clock and the dancers arrived at noon.

It was hard to imagine that homely Annie with her housekeeper's apron and washer-woman's hands had ever been one of these sirens. All sporting a uniform of bright red lipstick and various items of animal print, the nine muses minced their way down the central aisle to the hall. Their heels marched in time to the beat of their hips. One of the muses stopped by my nephew and gently walked her fingers down the side of his face.

"Wow, those eyes, they see right through yah! What's your name, handsome?"

"Luke" he spluttered.

"People call me Tilly. See you around, Luke." She stroked his chin and winked before turning to catch up with her colleagues.

"'Ere, Luke. Why don't you 'elp me check on the bell tower and let the ladies settle in?"

Phil guided my mesmerised nephew to the opposite end of the church. Despite the distractions, the rest of the preparations went off like a well-planned military operation. Barbara made sure that everyone had plenty of tea and cake. The florist from Market Square busily weaved her way up and down the central aisles attaching white orchids to the end of the benches, tutting as she went about not needing all of this 'aggro' on the busiest day of the year.

The flowers looked stunning though. A large display of calla lilies was already in place in front of the altar. More flowers would arrive with the hearse, along with the funeral party.

By one o'clock, the church was full. Arabella had requested that the undertakers did all the heavy lifting, so Leo led his sons and four other staff members as they carried in the ornate walnut coffin, also covered with a bouquet of white orchids and lilies. Arabella drew on all her former acting experience to deliver an extremely touching eulogy. Her son Tristan read out a self-penned poem in honour of his grandfather. It wasn't a great verse but was heartfelt. I was quite in awe of his confidence, a trait he obviously inherited from his mother, though his amphibian features sadly showed his looks came from his absent father. Then it was time for the Muses.

The intoxicating sound of lyres and flutes, harps and tambourines bounced off of the stone walls and wooden eaves as the nine dancers leapt and spun their way, barefoot, around the abbey. Each of them was dressed in a different coloured robe, the flowing material cinched at the waist with a golden rope. In their hands, they carried a symbol or prop to identify their role; one had a lyre, another a scroll, one a mask and so on. They lay them down at the foot of the altar, gathered around the coffin and joined hands. As the power of the music swelled, the muses skipped around Lord Somerstone's body, before finally fainting to the floor in an act of unified grief.

The shocked congregation didn't know if they should clap or not. It was a breath-taking performance but this was a funeral. My aunt Cindy led the way. Standing up she encouraged everyone to applaud. Genuinely humbled by the standing ovation, the Muses took their bows and comforted each other as they retired to the wings. This had clearly been an emotional experience for them too.

A light drizzle of rain started on cue as the funeral procession left the church and made its way up to the Somerstone family tomb at the far end of the graveyard. The resident cat community stared out blankly from the headstones at the solemn parade. Arabella stoically walked proudly behind the coffin; her arm linked through Tristan's. There were no tears. No hysteria. Just a dignified silence. Behind the immediate family walked Ralph and Annie, both seemingly numbed by the whole experience, they appeared to be holding each other up. Many Islanders were there to honour a life well-lived. Whatever the morality of his pastimes, no one could deny that the late Lord Somerstone has taken life and squeezed out every drop of pleasure it had to offer.

As the coffin neared the mausoleum, the Muses broke line and skipped ahead to arrange themselves in a tableau around the tomb. Their coloured robes were now slightly more revealing due to the effect of the rain. Leo Peasbody strode to the front, pulled open the mausoleum doors and walked inside. The funeral party halted, and I prepared myself to lead the final part of the ceremony.

Suddenly, one of the Muses, I think it was Tilly - she had positioned herself closest to the front, let out a scream loud enough to wake the nearby residents. Leo reappeared, obviously agitated, and slammed the tomb doors together. Slumped against them, he looked anxiously across to Arabella and shook his head.

"I'm sorry," he said. "Can somebody call the police. I think I have found Gordon Wright!"

Back to Base

P hil offered to stay with Leo to stand guard whilst the rest of the shocked funeral party stumbled back to the church. My mother stepped forward and syphoned off a quivering Arabella to the vicarage. In a similar vein, Luke proved himself to be the man of the hour by taking a dazed Tristan off to my study to download a computer game. Barbara marched everyone else to the hall for refreshments and the pallbearers placed Lord Somerstone's coffin back in front of the altar. Sam came back to the vestry with me to await the arrival of the police.

"How long do you think Gordon's body has been there?" I asked as I rehung my vestments in the wardrobe.

"Well, he certainly wasn't there last night!" Sam seemed to blush. "I helped Leo open up the tomb. And I promise you there were no extra bodies. Someone must have put him in after we left."

"And that was around what time?"

"Erm, I'm not sure. It was dark."

I looked askance at my friend. I sensed there was something she wasn't telling me. Then I noticed something was missing.

"I thought we made a pact to always wear our earrings. Didn't they go with your outfit?"

"What? Yes, sorry, Jess. Er, my bad, I just put in the pearl studs without thinking."

She looked anxious.

"'Hey, I'm joking! It's only a pair of earrings. It would be crazy to never wear anything else. As long as you haven't lost them!" I laughed.

Sam started to pick at some dropped candle wax on the top of the chest of drawers.

"Of course not! Let's go get some tea. You must be gasping. Then we had better check in on Arabella. Such a shock, poor dear. I really feel for her."

"She really has had a traumatic few weeks. Money can't buy happiness, eh?"

About an hour later PC Taylor and a couple of his colleagues from the mainland search patrol were gathering witness statements from everyone in the hall. Inspector Lovington had taken the rest of the team to the graveyard. Sam and I gave our statements and headed to the vicarage to see how Arabella and Tristan were bearing up. Cindy greeted us at the door.

"I have given Arabella something to help her relax. Darling, I hope you don't mind but your Mum said she could lie down in your room. Luke is looking after Tristan. There is something terribly sad about that boy. It breaks my heart to see such darkness in the eyes of one so young."

I wasn't sure if Cindy was referring to Tristan or my nephew, maybe it was just a teenage boy thing. I peeked into the study on my way to the kitchen and both of them looked happy enough, their dark eyes illuminated by the blue screen in front of them.

"Where's Zuzu?"

"Refreshing her makeup, I think," Mum replied. "I imagine Dave will be over here to get her statement shortly."

I thought it might be a good opportunity, with my sister out of the room, to do a little more digging around what my aunt knew about Dave Lovington's past.

"So, Cindy, you never mentioned anything before to me about Inspector Lovington's wife or her death. Mum tells me she committed suicide. When I pushed you on how you knew each other in the pub a few weeks ago you said it wasn't your place to say anything."

"It's not. Well, okay, I admit. I didn't say anything to you, my darling girl, because I thought you and he might, you know, and that it wasn't right to tell you he was a widower before, you understand."

"Not sure that I do, but please continue. Why did she kill herself and what has any of that got to do with you?"

My line of questioning was, perhaps, a little too direct but my aunt could be very evasive.

"Darling, why does anyone want to take their own lives? She was desperately unhappy."

"But she had a gorgeous husband, and two beautiful children. I am guessing they had money."

"Money doesn't buy you happiness, remember." Sam reminded me.

"Yes, they had money. Everything looked perfect. That's what Dave couldn't understand either. But she was very ill. She couldn't see any other way out of the pain. That's what he wanted to know, and I helped her explain herself to him."

"Aunt, please enough. You can't speak to the dead. No one can. Be honest, you just told him what he needed to hear. I understand that. People need some comforting words when they are grieving."

"So, you don't believe in an afterlife? Darling, isn't that the whole point of your job!"

"Don't be facetious, you know that is not what I meant at all. Of course, there is an afterlife. I just don't believe there's a celestial FaceTime messaging system."

"You need to open your heart, my darling child. Bev told me you had a vision. Just give it time. All will be revealed."

If having visions was going to leave me faint and gasping for breath, I think I would be better off keeping my heart firmly closed. Talking of my closed heart, a few minutes later our conversation was interrupted by the arrival of Inspector Lovington, fresh from the scene of the crime. He was followed closely behind by Zuzu, totally milking the distressed damsel angle. Gently dabbing at her eyes with a handkerchief, being very careful not to smudge her mascara, my sister slid herself into the chair opposite Dave. His bashful smile registered the impact of her performance.

"I need to speak with Lady Somerstone-Wright. Where can I find her?"

"Dave, darling, I am afraid I gave her a little something to calm her nerves. She is resting upstairs. I am sure you will be able to speak to her in a while. Why don't you take all of our statements first? I am sure whatever you have to tell her can wait. I doubt Mr Wright is going anywhere."

"And a cup of tea? Have you had lunch? Zuzu, I believe there is some of yesterday's casserole in the fridge. You can warm that through." My mother motioned to Zuzu to get up and look after her man, fluttering eyelashes were not going to keep this army marching.

"Inspector, I hope you don't mind, but I need to get back to the hospital. I have already given my statement to PC Taylor." Dave nodded and Sam quickly made her goodbyes before slipping out of the back door.

I had a feeling she wasn't rushing straight to the hospital.

Dunkirk

The rain persisted through the afternoon and the pathways through the graveyards grew slippery from the repeated toing and froing of the police forensic team. A second team from the mainland brought portable floodlights with them and the investigation went on till late in the night.

After the statements of the funeral guests were taken, a carriage was sent to collect Arabella and Tristan about eight o'clock. The last ferry had left for the day and many of the guests now had nowhere to spend the night. I gave instructions to Phil to keep the heat on in the church and let the police have full use of the hall until further notice. In response, Barbara and Rosemary rallied a team of volunteers to gather bedding and other essentials to keep the officers and guests fed and watered. The Muses, unable to return to their club, mucked in and a reassuringly British Dunkirk spirit took over.

"Reverend, I don't suppose you have seen Lawrence Pixley?"

"No, not at all, Inspector. I haven't seen him all day. Why do you ask?"

"Am I right in thinking you said he had a monogrammed handkerchief with the initials L.P."

"Yes. Every time I have seen him, he has been using one. I imagine they're a present from his mother. People rarely buy such gifts for themselves. He always seems to have a cold."

"Yes, well. As you say, probably a gift from his mother. And a man with his initials on a handkerchief might well have his initials on other personal items."

"What like a wallet? Tie? Yes, I suppose they would."

"And you are sure you haven't seen him today?"

"Yes, I am sure. But it is a school day. I imagine he was at work and then went home. There is absolutely no reason for him to be here."

"No, you are right, of course. Thank you, Reverend."

I suspected there was a motive behind the Inspector's questions, and I had to find out more. I sensed that he thought that Lawrence was somehow involved in Gordon's death.

"Inspector, Dave? Have you found something?"

Dave pulled me to the back of the church and took out a couple of evidence bags from his pocket. "Jess, Mrs Reynolds mentioned in her statement that she had seen a tall fair-haired man entering the churchyard yesterday evening. Her exact words were that he looked 'shifty'. Mrs Reynolds didn't see his face clearly, but that description would match the headmaster. Now, what reason would Mr Pixley have to be visiting a graveyard in the dark? He was the only person to claim that Gordon Wright went back to Bridewell Manor last Tuesday. The security guard and staff all say they didn't see him return that evening. We have reliable witness testimony and his own statement confirming that he and Mr Wright had a fight. And I really shouldn't do this but, we found these on the ground underneath Mr Wright's body. See the cufflink has the initials L.P. — Lawrence Pixley."

"May I?" I carefully took the bags by their corners and lifted them up to the light for a better view. The mother of pearl cufflink clearly had the initials L.P. engraved in gold lettering. Inside the second bag, though, was a familiar blue earring. "Inspector, before you arrest Lawrence Pixley, I think you might want to talk to Dr Hawthorne."

A Flock of Seagulls

A fter a heart-warming communal breakfast in the hall with the Abbey's funeral refugees, I set off on my usual Saturday morning rounds, including my regular visit to the Cottage Hospital. This morning's coffee with my best friend was going to be very, very interesting.

"Before you say anything, I wasn't sure where I had lost the earring. I knew I would find it."

"Where? When? How long were you cavorting in the crypt? Seriously, Sam!"

"Don't you dare judge me! We didn't. You know. We just had a little, er, embrace."

"Quite the *embrace* to dislodge an earring, *and* a cufflink."

"What can I say, behind that solemn facade lies a man with uncontrollable passions."

"Obviously. Don't you have any self-control? You're the senior practitioner here. Think of your reputation."

"I do. Don't preach at me. I just," Sam sighed "... he's insatiable."

"And reckless. You almost got an innocent man arrested."

"Don't be dramatic! Anyway, how do you know Lawrence Pixley is innocent? You said the Inspector couldn't verify his statement that Gordon Wright went back to the manor house."

"I just do. Did you hear that the coroner has confirmed Gordon was stabbed in the back?"

"Yes, a sneaky death. A coward to not look your victim in the eyes. Sounds like Pixley to me. He's a bit of a mouse."

I wasn't sure why, but I didn't like Sam's attack on Lawrence's character. He was reserved but I agreed with Audrey Matthews he had a quiet integrity.

"Anyway, I guess you will get your earring back at some point."

I started to pack up my bag.

"One question that remains unanswered is where has Gordon been all this time? Leo says there was no blood in the mausoleum so he must have been killed elsewhere and bled out. It's been ten days. Without some form of refrigeration, he would've started to decompose."

"Well, I am sure the police will figure it out. They are clearing the scene today so we can finally lay Lord Somerstone to rest. I am going to take Cilla up to Bridewell now to talk arrangements through with Arabella. You don't suppose she did it, do you?"

"Her shock appeared genuine yesterday. I can't imagine a mother wanting her son to discover his father like that, can you?"

***

The drive up to the manor gave me time to think about Sam's words. I took a few moments to rest by the bench at the end of the drive that looks out across the harbour. I took off my helmet and shook my hair out. There was a gentle fog covering the bay beneath, though the sun was doing its best to warm the earth below. A seagull plopped down beside me with some snatched fish from the market. Soon he was joined by another and then another. All three fought over the tasty treat, squaring up to each other and then grabbing at the fish when they had the opportunity. Seagulls are the thugs of the bird world.

"So," I said to the gulls, "we know it wasn't Tony or Eric. It makes no sense, and they have alibis. Hugh Burton might have a motive but why now? Surely once her father passed away Arabella would seek a divorce. There was no need to kill her husband. And I know he got on that ferry with Freya. Arabella? I believe her. She didn't pretend to love Gordon, but he was still her son's father. I can't see her wanting the man dead. I am sure Lawrence is telling the truth. Surely a guilty man wouldn't admit to following his victim after their fight. It clearly makes him a suspect. The key question is, if Gordon went back to Bridewell, did he stay there? No one in the house admits to seeing him later that day. Maybe he didn't go back into the main house. Hugh was holed up on the pig farm, there must be other outbuildings too. Or did he sneak out again the same way he crept in? If Gordon went out again, I have no idea who the murderer could be. But if he didn't go out again then his murderer is someone at Bridewell Manor."

The gulls gave no reply.

"Anyway, thanks for listening. And guys, please play nice, okay?"

I straddled Cilla and, holding my helmet in my right hand, drove the few yards up to the gatehouse. The security guard took a quick look at my dog collar and buzzed me through.

The metal gates creaked open.

"Erm, sorry, just a quick question. How do members of the family get in when you aren't here?"

"They have remote overrides on their key fobs."

"So, they are able to come and go as they please and you wouldn't necessarily know if they did?"

"Of course, it's not a prison!" he grunted.

Ralph answered the door and led me into the dining room where Arabella and Tristan were having lunch.

"Reverend Ward, what a lovely surprise. Come. Join us. Have you eaten already? Annie makes a wonderful shepherd's pie, there's plenty to go around. Ralph, set up an extra place at the table for the vicar. Would you like some wine?"

"No thank you, it's a bit early for me, but I will join you for a bite to eat. It smells divine."

"Tris was telling me about the game he and, I'm sorry what was your nephew's name again?"

"Luke. He's my sister Rosie's son."

"Yes, Luke. Seems this computer game was, what did you call it Tris? 'Givenchy'?"

"Gucci." Tris corrected his mother. "It was Gucci. You are so old!"

"Gucci means good, right?" he nodded and buried his head in his meal. I felt quite proud of my knowledge of teenage slang. "Tristan, you can come over to play any time you like. You both seemed to get on well."

Tristan shrugged his shoulders and his frog-like eyes rolled to the back of his head.

"Mother, are we going to engage in small talk all through lunch? If so, I'd rather take this to my room."

"Tris! That is very rude! Apologise to the Reverend at once."

"I'd rather go to my room."

"Then go."

Tristan collected his plates and slithered out of the room.

Arabella broke down.

"What am I going to do? I don't know how to parent. He's been at boarding school since he was six. I have no idea how to speak to him. I hardly know my own son."

"He's a teenage boy; from what I have seen they are all like this. And he has just lost his father and grandfather. Just give him space. It's a lot to process. He is the man of the house now." I genuinely felt sorry for Arabella and instinctively knew she was not responsible for Gordon's death but felt strongly that someone at Bridewell was. "By the way, I hope you don't think me impertinent, but I am sure you have heard that Mr Pixley has given a statement to the police claiming that Gordon returned here the night he went missing, yet no one in the house says that they saw him. Arabella, do you have any reason to suspect they are lying? Has anyone been acting suspiciously?"

"Reverend! Are you trying to suggest that I, or a member of my household, murdered my husband!"

"I am sorry, I am not suggesting anything, just curious. Someone must know something." Ralph re-entered with my serving of Annie's shepherd's pie, and I quickly changed the subject. "Hmm, that smells delicious!"

Below Stairs

Without the presence of a brooding teenager and my probing questions, lunch passed by pleasantly enough considering the situation. We agreed to complete Lord Somerstome's entombment the next day after mass. I told Arabella that I could show myself out and made my way out into the main lobby. I remembered the first time I visited Bridewell Manor and was greeted by Arabella who talked about redoing the decoration. Her tastes were more minimalist than previous generations of her family, including her father. Looking around at the grandeur of the main entrance with its gold leaf and mirrored surfaces, I did think it would be a shame to rip all this out and start again. I suppose there is no point in getting sentimental over things. Each generation must make its own mark. Take Lord Somerstone himself, covering all those beautiful chairs with back copies of National Geographic. No wonder the floor was sticky. All that clutter would be impossible to clean.

My vision!

Oh my! What if the shadow I saw standing over Geoffrey Somerstone was Gordon Wright? What if the shadow folding in on itself was Gordon being stabbed in the back? Who could have stabbed him? Why didn't I see that, eh? What's the point of a visionary flashback that only shows you half the picture? That's the trouble with imaginary visions caused by too much sugar - they are complete nonsense! However, it is very possible that Lord Somerstone's bedroom was the scene of the murder.

I cast a quick look around to check no one was about and sneaked back up the corridor to the pink room. The smell of bleach remained overpowering. Someone had worked very hard to clean up any evidence. Maybe I could find a knife or some other clue. The reddy-brown circles! I pushed through the piles of papers and there they were.

Perhaps if I just squatted down, I could feel around on the floor. The killer might have missed something. I crawled around on all fours weaving my way through piles of old magazines and newspapers. I found nothing.

"Get a grip on yourself, Jessamy Ward. What nonsense! You didn't see anything, you silly old fool," I muttered, as I backed out towards the door.

"What exactly didn't you see, Vicar?"

I turned around to see Ralph and Annie standing at the entrance.

"See Ralph, I told you. When you told me about her fainting. I warned you. She *saw* 'something'. She's a Bailey. Lord Somerstone told us many a time about the Baileys. About Cynthia and her powers. We have to —"

"Hush now, my dear. We've nothing to be afraid of." Ralph pulled his wife to him and straightened up. His broad frame dwarfed the woman beside him. "Reverend Ward, please come with us."

I made a few feeble protests before nervously following them back down the hallway, through the reception and down the passage that leads to the kitchen. The sudden realisation that I could be walking 'below stairs' with Gordon Wright's murderers seized me, but something deep inside told me that everything would be fine.

"Please, sit down, Vicar. Annie put the kettle on. I think Reverend Ward will need a cup of tea."

It was beginning to make a little sense. The reddish-brown stain where the chair stuck. The powerful smell of bleach. That was the murder scene. The stain was dried blood. So, which one of them did it? Was it Annie? Her mild demeanour hid a rough start in life. She had been a dancer at the Aphrodite, notwithstanding being a 'muse' that was a tough profession and not one women from happy homes tend to enter. Could it have been Ralph, the loyal butler? He was ex-military. He would know how to creep up on a man and dispatch him quickly. But why? Did they learn about Gordon's plans to turn Bridewell Manor into a hotel? They both could lose everything if that happened. But Ralph didn't appear to have any knowledge of these plans when we spoke, though maybe Annie did. Or maybe Ralph did it to protect his master. In my vision the shadow was leaning over the bed. Was Gordon trying to hasten his father-in-law's end?

Annie placed a china cup and saucer in front of me and sat down next to her husband. Ralph placed both his palms face down on the table, took a deep breath and fixed me with his eyes.

"I know what you are thinking, Vicar, but we didn't kill Gordon."

"We wouldn't, we couldn't. Sweetheart, tell her. We loved all the family. They had been so good to us."

"Even Gordon?" I was confused.

"Even Gordon. He wasn't the nicest of men, but he meant no harm. He was just well —"

"A bit of a prick!"

"Annie!"

"Well, he was, Babe. I hate to speak ill of the dead but there you are."

I looked at the distraught couple, propping each other up. There was no way they took Gordon's life.

"So, if you didn't kill Gordon, who did? He couldn't have stabbed himself in the back."

Ralph looked at his wife and looked down at the table, shaking his head.

"There was only one other person in the room."

"Geoffrey Somerstone!"

My hands rushed to my mouth as if they were trying to push the words back in.

The couple nodded. They were serious.

"He used a letter opener."

Ralph's eyes began to mist up. He was betraying his master's memory and the words stuck in his throat.

"Babe, there-there now. I'll tell her." Annie stood up and going to a nearby drawer pulled out a blood-stained copy of The Times newspaper. Placed it on the table and unfolded it to reveal an ornate silver letter opener with the Somerstone family crest on its hilt. "Lord Somerstone liked to open all the mail in the evening. He had a routine, you see. He would rise around midday, Ralph would take him The Times and he would read it whilst he had breakfast, then Ralph washed and dressed him and after a light supper, Lord Somerstone would attend to business matters. As he grew weaker, he found this old family heirloom a great help in opening all his correspondence. It's quite sharp. He kept it by his bed. We are not sure exactly what happened. Ralph couldn't have been away for more than a few minutes."

"His Lordship preferred to read his mail alone. Business was a private matter. When I returned Gordon was lying on the floor in a pool of his own blood!"

"But his lordship told Ralph that it was self-defence."

"And you just accepted that? You didn't ask him any further questions? Why didn't you go for help?"

"The man was obviously dead!" Ralph's shoulders shook with the recollection. Annie put her hand on his to offer comfort.

"At Lord Somerstone's request, Ralph removed Gordon's body in his lordship's wheel-chair, and we kept him in the chiller out back. No one ever goes there."

"And you just followed orders. But, if it was self-defence, why didn't you just tell the police?"

"What and have his last few days spent handcuffed to a prison bed whilst Ernest Woodward argued to get him home on bail?" Ralph broke down. He wiped the tears and snot away on his arm. Annie sprang to her feet again and grabbed some paper towels, which she ripped in two and gave half to her husband.

"You see, Vicar. The attack seriously weakened his lordship. He begged Ralph to help him. It was surely only a matter of days, even hours. We thought we would tell people what happened after his death. We couldn't bring Mr Wright back."

"And Gordon usually wasn't here much. We really didn't think anyone would notice he was gone."

"I see, and then Arabella called the police. The stress you must have been under to keep the body concealed. Annie, was that why you didn't want me to get the ice?" Despite feeling slightly queasy at the thought that the ice for my drink had been sitting next to Gordon's rotting corpse, I found myself having enormous sympathy for the couple.

"Yes. I am sorry, Vicar."

"And the smell of bleach in the sick room, that was to clean up after the stabbing."

"Yes, the blood splattered everywhere. I had to take several piles of newspapers and burn them in the furnace." Annie rubbed the table with the paper towel, unconsciously re-enacting the scrubbing motion of cleaning the blood away. Ralph now put his hand down on hers to calm her.

"But you missed a spot. On the legs of one of the chairs. I noticed small sticky circles when I was up there."

"Is that all you saw? Vicar, when you fainted the other day... you were frightened. I got a shock from you. Like a jolt. I thought, perhaps... But ... You didn't *see* anything else. You meant the bloodstains... That was what you saw."

Ralph appeared comforted by this version, so I let it ride.

"Yes, that's what I meant. You don't believe I have some special power, do you?"

"Of course not." They both laughed nervously. "That would be silly."

Yes, I thought, remembering my vision, the words at the well and Freya's phone call that mentioned the freezer — that would be very silly.

Don't Look Back in Anger

"Let me check I have got this right, you say that you couldn't live with the lies anymore so knowing that the mausoleum was being reopened on Thursday, you wheeled Gordon Wright's body up to the open tomb. You waited in the shadows until Mr Peasbody and Dr Hawthorne left and then placed Mr Wright's corpse on the floor of the tomb, knowing it would be discovered the next afternoon. That makes no sense. Why didn't you leave it where it was?"

Inspector Lovington had agreed to take Ralph and Annie's statements in the kitchen at Arabella's request. She didn't want the whole Island to witness her loyal servants being dragged into the incident room at the back of the Cat and Fiddle. She now stood with her hands on Annie's shoulders as she gave evidence.

"I don't know. I guess we panicked, what with young Tristan back in the house. I couldn't have him finding his father, could I?"

Though Ralph was a giant of a man he now appeared like a frightened child.

"You do realise that it is a crime to pervert the course of justice. I should charge you both with being accessories to murder after the fact."

"But it was self-defence, Inspector! They were trying to protect my father. I promise you, if you bring charges, I will hire for them the best attorneys money can buy."

"And what about wasting valuable police time, eh? We had nearly half the force combing the Island looking for Mr Wright and you had him in your chiller all along!"

"Yes, my husband. My chiller. Now, I hope you have enough information to proceed. I expect your utmost discretion in this matter, Inspector Lovington. I believe I know your father, Sir Nigel Lovington. Your older brother and I were extremely, hmmm, let's say intimate back in the day. I am sure you understand my most fervent desire to clear all this nasty business up as soon as possible."

The Inspector bowed his head and put his black notebook back in his breast pocket.

"I believe I do indeed have everything I need, Lady Somerstone-Wright. I bid you all a good day."

As I watched my sister's boyfriend turn to leave, I couldn't quite process what had just transpired. As he closed the door behind him, I looked at Arabella.

"Oh, don't you fret, Reverend. Dave Lovington is old-school. He understands what he needs to do. Come now, I think we all need a drink. Ralph, Papa's finest malt I think."

I leant across the table. "Arabella, don't you want to know why your husband attacked your father? Ralph must know more than he's saying?"

"Reverend. Jess..." Arabella fixed me with weary eyes, "What is the point of knowing? Will it change anything? If Papa had wanted me to understand he would have told Ralph. He didn't. Whatever it was, Papa wanted to protect me. I guess it was to do with money, or his business dealings or maybe he was drunk or all of the above. Who knows? And who cares? This isn't a 'whodunnit'. Bad things happen. They are both at peace now. I need to take care of the living. Ah, the whiskey!"

Ralph placed four crystal tumblers on the kitchen table. Arabella picked up her glass.

"Though, next time you need to dispose of a body, Ralph, might I suggest the pig barn. My darling little micros would have made short work of him." Dramatically slamming the glass down on the table Arabella then raised it high and called out "To my incredible Papa, Earl of Wesberry and lover of life!"

The three of us joined her in the toast.

"To Lord Somerstone, may he rest in peace!"

It's Getting Late

"**M**ummy, That's great news! We are going to have so much fun. I knew you wouldn't be able to tear yourself away. Not when all three of your beautiful daughters are here."

The squeals of excitement from my sisters hit me as I opened the vicarage door.

"Jess? Jessie, is that you? Mum's decided to stay."

"What I actually said was that I would look at the possibilities of moving back. If I can rent out my house..."

I threw my arms around my mother. Zuzu and Rosie moved in for a group hug. Families come in all shapes and forms I thought. This is mine and it's perfect.

"So," I suggested, "what does everyone think about lunch tomorrow at the Cat and Fiddle after mass?"

Taking this as her cue to extract herself from this mob of over-affection, my mother started to walk towards the kitchen.

"I'm up for that, the first round is on me. I will be toasting finally sealing Geoffrey into his tomb. Trust that old devil to have two goes at it!"

"And I will be toasting a new start for me and Luke. We were talking earlier, and he is happy to stay here until he heads off to university next year. He's actually quite excited."

"They don't have dancing girls at church every funeral you know, Lukey boy!" Zuzu opened the study door and called out to her nephew, who was glued to my computer.

"No." Rosie reached over and close the door again. "He wants to make that attic space into a gaming den. Not gambling, Jess. Oh, the look on your face! No, PCs, consoles and the like."

There was a distinct air of alcohol on their breaths.

"How much have you had to drink?"

"Don't worry Sis, we left you some. Had to keep Rosie company. Teddy's a total bastard, by the way. C'mon through to the kitchen. Did you know I'm dating a baron?"

"Fourth son of a baronet, actually. Yes, I did. And I also know who killed Gordon Wright. I have just been with your boyfriend as he closed the case."

"Wow, there's never a dull moment here, eh? Let's have some more wine and you can tell us all about it. Mum? Rosie? What's for dinner?"

"I have no idea, Zuzu dear, what are you cooking?"

I lingered in the hall for a while, watching my mother and sisters staggering off towards the kitchen, holding each other up physically and emotionally.

"I'll be there in a moment. I've just got to finish a few things before tomorrow."

I could hear Zuzu's voice in the distance saying something about all work and no play makes Jess a dull girl. As Luke was in the study, I walked into the morning room and sat down on the sofa. It had been a whirlwind couple of weeks. So many revelations. So much to take in. I was sure it would settle down but right now, I needed a quiet moment with the Boss-man. I closed my eyes. Slowed down my breath and centred myself for prayer. I had so much to be grateful for.

Through the walls, I could hear laughter from the kitchen. From the study beside me, there was the sound of laser guns. And in the distance, the foghorns alerted passing sea traffic to take care of the rocks off the western coast. The sun had given up on her mission to warm the earth and the fog had won, for today. Tomorrow, we would start again.

Sam was right. I didn't need a man. I had Jesus. I had my faith. I also had my family and friends. And I had Hugo.

"Hello buddy, here let me lift you up." I reached down to the furry slinky that had started to wrap himself around my ankles. "There, that's better." His black fur was soft and comforting. The moment was perfect.

Until I sneezed.

"Sorry, Hugo. I forgot to take my antihistamines." Within seconds my eyes were watering. As quickly as I picked him up, I had to drop him back down. "Now, where did I put them? Darn it, they must be in my room. Here, Hugo, come on. Go to the kitchen. I don't want to trap you in here."

Indignant at such degrading treatment Hugo just sat where I had dropped him. I stood in the doorway making mewing sounds to try and entice him out.

"Come on, Cat, I'm dying here. I have to get my tablets!"

There was a loud knock on the door. Who is it now?

"Coming!" I felt my way along the hall wall to the door. My eyes were now stinging rivers. "Who is it?"

"Frederico!"

"Who?"

I finally found the latch.

There in the fog stood a Brazilian god.

Tall. Tanned. Muscles. Moustache.

"I'm sorry, did you say your name was Frederico?"

"Sim, meu nome é Frederico."

Wow. I called for Zuzu to come to the door. "Sister, I think your luggage has arrived."

"Really, it's getting a bit late. Still... Oh My God! What are you doing here?"

"I take it you weren't expecting Frederico to call then, eh? You must invite him in. It's perishing cold out there."

Zuzu cast me the most vicious look. "Of course. Don't stand there on the doorstep. Come in. Come in. So, er, how did you find me?"

"Quero te surpreender. How do you say... Surprise!"

"Yes, oh I am surprised. I don't understand. This address, how did you find this house?"

"You left this." Frederico produced a postcard Freya had sent to her mother the very first day we arrived. It was a view of Harbour Parade and featured the cliff railway. It was the most unimaginative picture.

She had written *'Wish you were here, The Vicarage, Wesberrey.'*

"That's all you had to go on. Wow, pretty impressive. But, Freddy, I don't understand what you are doing here."

"I come to ask you." Frederico, the Brazilian god, all tan and muscles bent down on one knee. There was only one direction this conversation was going. "Case comigo, you will marry me?"

"I will marry you?"

"Yes? You say 'yes'!"

"No! I say 'NO'." Zuzu looked at me, her eyes popping. "Jessie, please help me!"

The End

What's Next for Jessame?

PIOUS POISON

Wrong Doers, it's time to say your prayers!

Jess Ward joined the Wesberrey Walkers to get fit. But it might be the death of her!

Obliged to look after her older sister's handsome and driven Brazilian lover, Jess introduces Frederico to the local walking group. With the annual Wesberrey Walkathon a few weeks away, everyone has their sights on the prize, but is there someone in the group prepared to kill for it?

A mysterious illness lays low several walkers and Jess suspects foul play. Who would deliberately poison their competition, and how did they do it? Still unsure of the reality of her newly discovered psychic abilities, but with little else to go on, Jess tries to channel help from a higher plane.

Can Jess trust her own intuition? Who or what is bringing everyone to their knees? Is it a dodgy hummus, or a deadly human?

PENELOPE CRESS
STEVE HIGGS

GREENFIELD
PRESS

PIOUS
POISON

Printed in Great Britain
by Amazon